# THE GOLDEN EAGLE

The Golden Eagle © 2024 Patrick Ford

All Rights Reserved. No part of this book may be reproduced in any form or by any electronic or mechanical means including information storage and retrieval syst ems, without permission in writing from the author. The only exception is by a reviewer, who may quote short excerpts in a review.

This book is a work of fiction. Names, characters, places, and incidents either are products of the author's imagination or are used fictitiously. Any resemblance to actual persons, living or dead, events, or locales is entirely coincidental.

Printed in Australia

Cover and internal design by Shawline Publishing Group Pty Ltd

First printing: August 2024

Shawline Publishing Group Pty Ltd

www.shawlinepublishing.com.au

Paperback ISBN 978-1-9231-7204-3

eBook ISBN 978-1-9231-7215-9

Hardback ISBN 978-1-9231-7226-5

Distributed by Shawline Distribution and Lightning Source Global

*Shawline Publishing Group acknowledges the traditional owners of the land and pays respects to Elders, past, present and future.*

 A catalogue record for this work is available from the National Library of Australia

# THE GOLDEN EAGLE

## PATRICK FORD

*For my mother Hilda, who gave me the greatest gift of all – literacy.*

# THE RAPE OF XANLATA

## Santa Marta, Spanish Conquered Territory, 1530

Sebastian Alfonzo de Martinez looked with pride on his new house in the small town of Santa Marta in the Spanish-conquered territory that people would know one day as Colombia. The house possessed lavish decorations and space as befitted a man of his stature. After all, did he not have a commission from King Phillip II himself to conquer and bring to God the heathen peoples of this Spanish outpost?

As the representative of the King and of God, he had achieved his holy mission in record time. He had devastated and enslaved the natives and had bought them to God with fire and the sword, in the process enriching himself and Spain with gold and silver in abundance. Most of these precious metals were as graven images, almost certainly those of the pagan gods. They had melted these abominations down and turned them into ingots for transport to Spain. Even now, a galleon was loading. It would sail within the week. He intended to be on it, his work here almost completed. There was only one more task and tomorrow he would begin it: the subjugation of the last of the *Muisica* strongholds, *Xanlata*. He expected to do this without difficulty and sail homeward bound in a fortnight. He would return in a year or so; there was always more treasure to find and more of God's work to do.

## Xanlata, Spanish Territory, 1530

Sebastian Alfonzo de Martinez sat on a rocky outcrop and watched as the town burned below him. Screams of terror and the groans of the wounded filled the air. Down there his troops were looting the town and raping the women. They were not discriminatory, for they had been a long time away from their wives, and they spared few from their attentions. Only half a dozen of the younger and more attractive remained reserved for Sebastian and his officers.

As dusk fell on the burning town, the soldiers formed up the survivors. The soldiers would take them to Santa Marta to be used as slave labour in the town's expansion. The women would perform important work in the kitchens and bedrooms of the officers, the men would build the town and its gardens. There were plans for a Governor's mansion and a cathedral to the greater glory of God. Sebastian fully expected to return as that governor.

As he watched the column set off for Santa Marta, the approach of one of his junior lieutenants, Orlando de Mandrao, who carried an ornate wooden box with him, interrupted Sebastian's dreams of gubernatorial splendour. The box was small, but he struggled to carry it. He placed it on the ground beside Sebastian's feet and invited him to open it. He was wide-eyed with wonder.

The column had moved out along the valley. Only these two men remained. Sebastian knelt and opened the exquisitely carved box, the lid a perfect fit. He could not understand how these primitive heathens could perform work of such precision given the meagre tools they used.

As his eyes fell on the contents of the box his heart leapt and his senses were almost overwhelmed. The image he lifted from the box was very heavy, almost certainly pure gold. It was an effort to lift it with two hands. He saw the statue of an eagle, wings folded, perched on an orb that was the biggest emerald he had ever seen. Two smaller emeralds served as the majestic bird's eyes. The whole thing was about a foot in height, and, in the reflected light of the burning town, it glowed with a lustre that was spellbinding. Avarice flooded Sebastian.

I must have this, he said to himself, I must. He turned to his lieutenant. 'Who else has seen this?' he demanded.

'No one else sire, I have only just discovered it. The men took all the other gold objects from the building; they left this, thinking, perhaps, that it was nothing more than a wooden box.'

'You have done well. See that no other knows about this. I will take it home to the King. It is fitting that he should have the most pleasing thing in all the world.'

They mounted their horses and followed the straggling column of soldiers and prisoners. The trail they took led through a high pass in the mountains before descending to the town of Santa Marta on the plains below. As they rode, Sebastian could not take his mind from the contents of the box strapped to his saddle.

The large emerald itself was worth a fortune. How much could he do, could he become, with such wealth? Any woman in Spain would be his, any high office he desired. He must have it for himself!

It was a long ride, and the soldiers were tired. They had spent much energy and adrenalin in the fighting and the rape and pillage that followed. None spared a thought for the natives; after all, they were doing them a favour, bringing them to the one true God and the promise of eternal life. Many had vied with each other to see how many women they could violate; they were now entering that state of detachment that exhaustion brought just before sleep overtook them, and they struggled with their stupor. Any who fell asleep on duty could expect the lash but still they were less than alert, completely unaware of what might happen behind them.

As they climbed into the high pass, the trail fell away to a dizzying gorge down which the swift river cascaded from rapid to rapid. A sudden idea struck Sebastian. *Now was his opportunity to gain ownership of the treasure.* He stopped his horse. 'He may have a stone in his hoof, I will check,' he said to Orlando as he dismounted.

His companion halted beside him to wait. He too got down to ease his saddle soreness and stood while Sebastian checked the hoof. Sebastian rose from his crouch and looked at his lieutenant. 'I am sorry, *mi amigo*, but you have seen too much. You must go to God with your knowledge,' he said, drawing his sword.

The surprised Orlando was slow to react. The sword plunged into his side, and he fell to his knees, still trying to understand what was happening. Sebastian withdrew his weapon and, with a swift kick, propelled the younger man over the edge. Panting with his effort, he leant on his sword until he recovered his composure. Orlando had fallen with hardly a sound, shocked into silence by his sudden demise.

Sebastian looked through the saddlebags on the now riderless horse. He removed most of the gold he found and placed it in his own saddlebags. He felt sorry for the horse for he had done no wrong, but he could not leave him alive now; Orlando's fate must look authentic. He struggled with the animal as it fought frantically to maintain its footing before it plunged into the abyss to join its rider in the valley far below.

Sebastian opened the box and lifted out the statue again. The brilliant emerald glowed in the faint moonlight. 'You are mine,' he said aloud. 'You will bring me fortune and fame. Anything is worth possessing you, anything!' Suddenly, he recoiled in horror. The green eyes of the eagle seemed to swivel towards his face, a baleful look in them, as if condemning him for his avarice and fratricide. They appeared to be saying, 'You have me now, but I will be your demise.' He almost dropped the magnificent bird in his shock as he felt the icon's condemnation deep in his soul. Quickly, he put it back in the box and tried to compose himself. But a feeling of dread that would never leave him assailed him. He had sold his immortal soul for a box of treasure.

When they reached Santa Marta, Sebastian reported the death of his lieutenant to the commander of the garrison. By the time they despatched a burial party to find the body, its journey through the rapids and waterfalls of the Rio Gonzo and the depredations of predators had removed any evidence of how the unfortunate Orlando had met his end. In any case, Sebastian was now at sea and would not reach Spain for many months.

After a long and tempestuous voyage, they approached the great harbour of Cádiz; Sebastian's sumptuous home in Granada lay a day's march away. He left the ship on a glorious spring day and assembled his retinue of servants to begin the last stage of his long journey. In Granada awaited his wife and children, whom he had not seen for over five years.

On the homeward journey, he had been loath to open his box; the feeling of dread still travelled with him. He had taken aboard one of the young captives from Xanlata. She had an unpronounceable native name and spoke no Spanish. He had named her Rosa and had availed himself of her supple body almost daily on the voyage. She displayed little emotion and was compliant as he used her, but her dark eyes were unreadable.

One day he finally opened the box and took out the statue to admire it. It relieved him to see no sign of the contempt he had seen in the emerald eyes; perhaps he had imagined it in the aftermath of his killing frenzy, but still the dread remained in the recesses of his mind. He had demonic dreams in which everyday events mixed with horrors unimaginable. Demons and goblins merged with hellfire and the staring eyes of his victims, Orlando, and the countless natives he had put to the sword, burnt at the stake or raped without mercy. Always the gleaming emerald eyes of the golden eagle roamed through these dreams, watching him with contempt. He would awake in a heavy sweat despite the cold, trembling in fear.

Sebastian dreaded going to sleep. He looked drawn and thin, for he had little appetite for the unappealing food on board. He began to drink heavily, hoping the wine would give him dreamless sleep. His companions remarked on his condition, but he ignored them. Some of them thought that his dusky travelling companion was too demanding and contributing to his emaciation. They hid jealous smirks, but he was too senior to them for any familiarity; after all, he had the ear of the Royal Court and could call down vindictive retribution upon them.

One evening, as they neared the straits of Gibraltar, greed tempted him to open the box again. He lifted the gleaming eagle and placed it on a bench. In its eyes there was no sign of the malignance he had seen before. He reached out to stroke it just as Rosa entered the cabin. Her eyes fell on the bird and she screamed in naked terror. She covered her eyes and turned away. She began calling out in her native tongue, seemingly crying for help, or praying to some higher being. Suddenly, she seized Sebastian's dagger from the side table and backed away toward the door of the cabin, finally turning to flee to the upper deck.

For a moment he hesitated, then followed her. When he emerged from below, he saw her, high on the poop deck, raising her arms to the heavens and screaming manically once more. She saw him and directed a stream of what sounded like invective at him.

He called out to her, but she seemed not to hear him. Still weeping, calling a plaintive prayer, she stabbed her arms and bare legs with the dagger, before plunging it into each of her eyes and leaping from the deck into the sea.

He turned to see a group of sailors, led by the chaplain, crossing themselves and averting their eyes. The priest, his eyes ablaze with religious fervour, held aloft his crucifix. 'I knew it to be so,' he cried. 'These women are witches, spawn of the devil. They lead you into temptation. We must destroy them.' He turned to his companion priests. 'See to it; remove the abomination from this vessel. Only then will we be able to enter the gates of Heaven!'

They hurried below, seeking three more Indian girls the crew had loaded on board for their convenience, and dragged them weeping to the deck. Still waving the crucifix and muttering imprecations, the priest ordered them all to be cast overboard. No one lifted a hand in their defence. The crew crossed themselves again, and with downcast eyes, went about their business.

Down in his cabin, Sebastian once more looked upon the statue. The eyes were gleaming in the light from the oil lamp, but there appeared to be no malice in them. Hurriedly, he put the bird back in the box and closed the lid. Was there a last glare in those eyes? He dared not open the box again.

Sebastian Alfonzo de Martinez reached his home the day after they had docked in Cadiz. He was feeling feverish, his head ached and he could not eat. He greeted his family, but apologised for his illness, attributing it to the arduous journey and his disrupted sleep, and made his way to his bed.

Before he did so, he concealed the box in a secret cavity in his bedroom wall. He told no one of its whereabouts.

Two weeks later he died from the typhus.

# A FLEETING FORTUNE

*Málaga, Spain, 1936*

Eduardo Alfonzo de Martinez bore no resemblance to his illustrious forebears. He was a small weasel-like man with nothing behind him except the dwindling remains of a substantial fortune.

For four hundred years, misfortune had dogged his family. When Sebastian Alfonzo de Martinez met his sudden death in Granada, it left his wife with some serious problems. She had spent a sizeable amount of the family fortune on extensive renovations to the grand home and had been depending on her husband to return with the fortune he had written about. The possessions he carried on his return contained some gold and jewels, but nothing like what she had needed to satisfy her creditors.

That was the least of her problems, for during the last year she had been carrying on an illicit relationship with a sea captain from *Genoa* whom she had met entirely by chance. Long deprived of her husband's services, she took lovemaking to new heights of passion and frequency with this seafarer. However, two weeks ago, she had made the devastating discovery that she was with child. While this worried her, she was confident she could pass off the child as her husband's, but his demise had ruined that plan. She had written to her lover in Genoa, but he had not replied; in fact, he made a very conscious decision to avoid Spanish waters for the near future.

When she could no longer hide her condition, she approached her husband's parents and asked for help. They refused her, broadcast her condition, shamed her. Her husband's family repossessed the house and all its contents and cast her out on the streets. Her own parents disowned her in their shame.

She could only return to the docks, hoping her lover would return – in the meantime, she eked out a living as a prostitute. She had been unlucky, for she miscarried a month after she had made the baby's presence known; no one had needed to know after all. She died in poverty seven years later of syphilis.

Her two daughters, taken in by their grandparents, married minor farming gentry and passed into obscurity. Her son could keep his title, and he found employment at the Royal Court as a minor diplomat, courtesy of a favour from a long-time friend of the family.

By the middle of the nineteenth century, the de Martinez family was in a crisis. A succession of bad political associations, unsuccessful speculation in the spice trade, and the financing of a succession of naval craft, most destroyed in various wars by the English and French, finally had the family facing penury. They sold the grand house in Grenada and moved to the coastal town of Málaga.

Somewhere along this road to financial disaster, employees discovered the box containing the golden eagle while demolishing the old wall containing the hidden cavity. The box, nailed shut and looking tattered after its long incarceration, went to the lady of the house, the Donna Madelina, who was only semiliterate in her knowledge of precious items. She did not open it and placed it in a storage room. It did not occur to her or the workmen to speculate on its obviously disproportionate weight. It went to the house in Málaga with the other belongings and left to rot.

Eduardo Alfonzo de Martinez had employment as the concierge of a large hotel in Málaga, much frequented by émigré White Russians and conservative politicians almost entirely aligned with the right-wing Falange.

So, it was with great trepidation that he awoke one morning and found his country embroiled in a bloody civil war and his city in the hands of the left-wing Republicans. This was a problem for Martinez. For a start, his aristocratic name would attract hostility, and if they discovered his family's long history of repressing the proletariat, he would be in much deeper strife. He debated whether he should go to work. Finally, he mustered the courage to telephone the hotel.

A coarse female voice answered, 'Seventh People's Front Headquarters, who is this?' He hung up. Outside, the streets looked calm, but there was almost no traffic and few pedestrians. Some trucks passed by, bearing armed men in the back, and flying red banners. He was in serious trouble.

What should he do? The hotel was out of the question, but somehow, he had to get out of the city. Eduardo would have to abandon the house and take only what he could carry with him. He would need money, and he had little of that; he searched the house to see if he could find more. There was some jewellery handed down from generation to generation, mostly silver with small emeralds and a few diamonds. He found some old currency notes and had to hope they were still legal tender. He packed a small case with clothes and toiletries and finally went to the basement to see what was there.

He uprooted old furniture, oil lamps, sacks of rotting clothing and boxes of old documents from long-defunct family business ventures. Eventually, in a corner, he discovered the box. *I wonder what is in that,* he mused. *Could it be of value?*

The box was old and rotting, and when he tried to move it, it disintegrated. He picked up one nail that had closed the box, made of iron, hand-formed. *This must be ancient,* he thought. He removed the wood and saw an object wrapped in rotting straw. When he had cleared away the packing, he could see that it was a figurine with a dull glow about it. He tried to move it and its weight surprised him. Gradually, he dragged it into the light of a basement window and gazed with mounting excitement at the eagle. It was gold and had several stones as well.

Finally, he picked it up and cleaned the remaining dust from it. He whistled at the dull lustre of it and the great orb of the emerald. It was very heavy. *It must be gold,* he thought. *I am rich!* Then realisation that he could do nothing with his find replaced his euphoria with a bitter disappointment.

He could not get it out of the building undetected. He could not carry it for long; it was far too heavy, and he had no motor car. He decided to secrete it somewhere in the house and return for it after things returned to normal; Eduardo felt sure the war would soon end, so he racked his brains for a location before deciding he would conceal it in a disused fireplace. He pushed into the opening and found several loose bricks high in the firewall. He removed these and placed the bird, wrapped in linen, into the space. He cleaned the fireplace, leaving no trace to show there was anything in there that should not be there.

He had experienced a moment of terror as he completed his task. He had placed the statue on a table and cleaned it with a polishing cloth. When he had finished, he noticed the gleaming emerald eyes. They seemed almost alive, looking benignly at him from the table, but when he wrapped the statue in the linen cloth, he could have sworn that the eyes changed; they appeared to swivel towards his face and adopt a look of such frightening malice that he almost dropped it in his shock. He must have imagined it, he reasoned, but the look remained with him for a long time. Many times, he remembered it and shivered with apprehension.

By now he was starving and craving coffee, so he decided to try to make his way out of the town. He took what valuables he had gathered, made his way to the street and headed towards the *estación*. There was still scant traffic, but in the distance, he could hear the rattle of rifle fire. Eduardo was not a brave man. He was a poor physical specimen and harboured a suspicion that he was a coward, so he moved towards the *estación* with a degree of trepidation.

He passed the hotel and noticed it festooned with red banners, and there were two men with red armbands and rifles guarding the door. The banners, emblazoned in black, outlined with yellow, proclaimed ¡*Viva la República!* Just around the corner, it terrified him to find the body of the Falange party secretary, who had frequently visited his hotel, hanging from a lamppost. He was wearing a placard around his neck that proclaimed *Enemigo de los Pueblos*. Eduardo wanted to return home immediately, but he reasoned he had come this far. He should proceed. The *estación* was only a few hundred metres away.

When he arrived, two large women with red armbands, pistols and coarse facial hair accosted him. 'Who are you? Where do you think you are going?' one demanded. He was careful to shorten his name.

'I am Eduardo Martinez and I live here in Málaga. I am hoping to travel to Granada to visit my grandmother.'

The two women laughed at him. 'There are no more trains to Granada, and you will not be going there until we have liberated it from the Fascists. You *will* go on a train to Barcelona, however. You are going to be a soldier of the people and fight the Fascists.'

'But I don't want to be a soldier. I have no political inclinations. I don't want to fight anybody. I just want to see my family.'

'*Ven con nosotros*,' one said, grabbing him by the arm and frogmarching him toward the sounds of musketry he had heard earlier. They reached the plaza central.

Across the square was a high masonry wall, pockmarked with many holes and about a dozen youths lined up against it. A firing squad composed of men wearing red armbands awaited the signal to fire. An officer gave the order; the rifles blazed, and the line of youths fell to the ground spouting gouts of blood. A man dressed in the uniform of an army officer, but without insignia save for a red armband, walked along the line of bodies and executed those still moving with his pistol.

'Those boys did not want to be soldiers, either,' said one woman. 'As a people's commissar, I have the authority to have you executed if you do not join us in our struggle.' Without a word, Eduardo took the proffered red armband and followed the women to the *estación*.

## Barcelona, Spain, 1936

The long and dirty train ride was enervating for Eduardo. He tried to sleep, but at every town and siding the train stopped while they made revolutionary speeches, and he and the others had to detrain to the cheers of the people. Girls placed flowers in their coat pockets and kissed them. *That part was good*, recalled Eduardo; *more girls than in his entire life had kissed him today.* They billeted them in a football stadium in *Barcelona*, every entrance heavily guarded to prevent these heroes of the proletariat from voluntarily discharging themselves from the army of the people.

In the morning, they marched to a military barracks laid to waste by the Republicans in their takeover of the city. There were still bloodstains and bullet holes in the walls and floors and prisoners in the cells.

For the next two weeks, they listened to the cries of the prisoners as guards interrogated them. Each morning at dawn there was the rattle of a firing squad. Four weeks of training was enough. NCOs taught them to drill, how to fire a rifle, how to apply a field dressing and throw a grenade. The front needed as much cannon fodder as it could get. Franco's troops were arriving by the shipload from Africa daily.

## Málaga, Spain, 1936-7

They entrained for Málaga in late September. Eduardo was glad to be going back there; he figured he would be close to the seaport and the Nationalist lines; both might provide an opportunity to desert.

Málaga had changed in the time he had been away. There were barricades in the streets. The streetcars ran infrequently, and many shops and bars had closed. The commanders and commissars took no chances with these reluctant heroes and marched them west out of town to the network of trenches defending the city. They had little equipment. They had received some leather belts with cartridge pouches and a small water bottle for each. It would be as nothing against the storm to come.

Christmas was a miserable time. The commissars frowned at any outward show of religion. It rained frequently and became very cold. They had little winter clothing, and the men complained. After the commissars had two men executed for anti-socialist dissent and spreading disaffection, the complaints ceased.

Meanwhile, Franco's forces received reinforcements and there were several squadrons of Italian aircraft on hand to support his troops.

The Republicans had failed to secure the airfields soon enough and most of the Spanish aircraft were flown away by their crews, who were sympathetic to the Fascist cause. There was virtually no Republican air force until the Russians arrived much later.

In early January, Franco began a heavy bombing of the Republican trenches. Unchallenged in the air, the Savoia-Machetti SM-79 bombers of the Italians caused havoc in the trenches. Many men tried to run, forced back at gunpoint by the NCOs. Commissars even shot some. The rest huddled in the trenches and watched as the bombs systematically destroyed both men and ammunition, as well as the few pieces of artillery they possessed. The Republicans were woefully unprepared. They had expected Franco to attack Madrid and had concentrated their forces there. Eduardo's plan was to avoid combat and surrender to the Fascists at the first opportunity, and it worked like clockwork. The Nationalist troops charged through the trenches of the Republicans and drove them in disarray right back to the street barricades where there was a more spirited resistance.

Eduardo removed his red armband and crouched in a hide he had scraped out of the trench wall, dragging several of his dead comrades across the entrance to conceal him. Night fell, and he could hear the battle fading away to the east, but during the night the SM-79s returned to bomb the city several times. Just before dawn, he could hear the voices of approaching troops. Their careless, casual conversation told him they were Nationalist soldiers mopping up.

After a time, Eduardo took a chance and called for help. He remained in his hide, but called out loudly, '*Ayúdame*, help me, I am a Nationalist soldier!' He heard them approach. 'If you are in that hole, come out with your hands up. Do not play any tricks on us. *Te vamos a matar*, we will kill you.' Eduardo carefully came out of the hole. He saw a sergeant and five Nationalist soldiers with rifles trained on him. They laughed at him. '*¿Dónde está tu uniforme?* You are a Republican!'

'I have no uniform,' he said. 'They picked me up from my house in Málaga and forced me to go with them. Take me to an officer. I have valuable information.'

They discussed his situation. Most of them still wanted to kill him, but he took the emerald jewellery from his pocket and offered it to them. 'If you spare me, these are yours, ¿*entiendes?*' The Sergeant looked at the emeralds. His uncle was a jeweller in *Valencia* and he could recognise good stuff when he saw it. 'Okay,' he said, 'we will find our *teniente*.' They took him towards the west.

*Teniente* Luis Escardo was a committed Fascist, on the way up. He was interested in what Eduardo had to say about the Republicans, their positions, strength, morale and weapons. But this was not enough. 'We already know all this,' he said. 'You must give me something else, or it will force me to send you back with the other prisoners. You have no uniform and were found in the enemy trenches. I am afraid we will shoot you.'

Eduardo said, 'Please ask your sergeant to leave us alone. I cannot speak in his presence.' The officer motioned to the man to leave the tent.

Eduardo had to play his last card. 'If you spare me, I will take you to a treasure I have concealed in my home in Málaga. A treasure so magnificent that there will be plenty for us both. We will share it.'

Luis did not believe him. '¡*Mierda!*' he said. 'Convince me. If it is as you say, we will truly share it and I will save your skin. I will place you with a section in my company to fight for Franco!'

Eduardo had no choice now. 'Will you give me your word as an officer and a gentleman?' he asked.

'Of course, you have my word.'

'¡*Excellente!*' said Eduardo. He told him all about the eagle and its hiding place. 'Thank you, sir, you will not be disappointed.

'I am sure that I will not be. '*Sargento*, this man is a Republican. He is trying to infiltrate our lines. Send him back with the other prisoners. It will be the firing squad for him!'

In the morning, they marched Eduardo to the wall behind the headquarters in a nearby farmhouse. He still could not comprehend what was happening to him. He could smell early orange blossom and hear birds calling. His last vision was of the malignant glare in the emerald eyes of the golden eagle.

# **EL CORONEL**

### Madrid, Spain, 1939

*Coronel* Luis Escardo, the former infantry *teniente*, was a cheerful man as he walked through the devastation of Madrid. At last, the war was over, Franco had won and would now establish a Fascist dictatorship that would last for many years. However, feelings still ran deep. Luis had prospered in the army. He had fought in several battles after Málaga, but it had been his transfer to the military police that had bought him fame and rapid promotion.

The Spanish Civil War was a bitter and divisive conflict, with no quarter given or asked. Violent opposing ideologies had driven both sides. There was torture, murder and rape, bombing of civilians, destruction on a large scale; both sides often executed prisoners. Terrible though it was, it was but a pale imitation of the war that would come to the world later that year.

### Madrid, Spain, 1940

*Coronel* Escardo was a legend in the military police. He had a burning hatred of the left wing, especially the communists, and any Russian prisoners who fell into his hands could expect no mercy. On one occasion, more than a hundred of his men repeatedly raped a female

Red Army commissar before she expired. He made several of her male companions watch before castrating them and turning them loose to bleed to death.

Luis treated offenders within his own ranks just as badly. His superiors, his soldiers and civilians alike knew him as *El muerte negro*, or the 'black death'. None addressed him by that name for fear of their lives, but he knew of this name and revelled in it.

He had retrieved the golden eagle from the house in Málaga soon after learning of it, but he was careful not to disclose his find to anyone. He partially unwrapped it for a quick look before he placed it in a sealed metal box and concealed it where he knew no one would ever find it.

He remained in his position with the military police until the Germans invaded and conquered France in June. Shortly afterwards, the general called him into his office. This exalted gentleman took him at once to the office of the Minister for the Interior, for the secret police were part of his portfolio. Many republicans still operated clandestinely, and they and the Basque separatists provided plenty of work for the 'forces of darkness', as the minister found it amusing to call his secret police.

'*Buenos dias Coronel,*' said the minister, 'we are pleased with your work. However, we have a new task for you. It is of the greatest importance and of utmost secrecy. Our German friend has shown remarkable progress in France. Our leader is thinking to join with him for there are some pleasant parts of southern France he would like to gain, not to mention Gibraltar and Portugal. However, he is biding his time. Our sources tell us der Führer has cast his eyes to the east, and we believe that is one battle he cannot win. But that is of no immediate concern to you. We have a pleasant interlude planned for you in Paris.'

Luis smiled. He had a special reason for visiting France, but he had told no one about it. 'What is it you require of me, minister?' he said.

'You will work with our friends, the Gestapo. They have expressed admiration for your success in extracting information from suspects. They want you to advise them and in return, they will provide us with some of their successful methods. There are many Basques in France, many of them known to you. Some of them have been working with the escape lines for downed British airmen. There could be significant advantages for us in this relationship. You will act as a civilian. There will be no paper trail to link you to us and you will have freedom of movement and action. Here are your orders. Memorise them and destroy them. Be prepared to leave by the end of the month.'

Since the end of the war, the Spanish borders had tight controls. The new government wanted to prevent left-wing elements from entering and wanted to apprehend those it saw as criminals arising from the war. For Luis, it meant that he could not even attempt to take his treasure out of Spain under the scrutiny of the border controls. Now he had a gift-wrapped opportunity. The highest sources would protect him from interference, for he had orders to move with utmost secrecy.

Luis was now almost forty years old. He had enjoyed his military career, and he lived a good lifestyle. Known and feared everywhere, he rarely had to pay a restaurant bill, and he could take his pick of women. The aura of power that surrounded him attracted some. Others agreed because of political blackmail or the threat of imprisonment. If all else failed, he could select one from the cells. He had never married; why would he bother?

## The Tomb at Convento de los Santos Benditos

He returned to his apartment and changed into casual clothes before walking several kilometres to a run-down garage whose proprietor was in his debt. A nondescript motor car awaited him; to any observer, he was just a middle-aged man taking a drive into the countryside. His destination was a ruined convent on the outskirts of Madrid.

In 1937, at the height of the Republican power, they had attacked many religious organisations, both for their wealth and in attempts to eliminate religion from the life of the new socialist society. The left appropriated precious artefacts, raped nuns, even crucified priests to their church walls. This convent had suffered such a fate. There was nothing left now but ruins, but Luis had discovered something when he brought some perpetrators back to face the scene of their crimes. There was an underground room in the building, inside the convent, walled up a century or more ago, but there was a secret entrance through a tunnel from a nearby crypt.

The superstitious, simple and rural folk avoided the ruins. Luis was careful to spread rumours of satanic rituals and curses placed on the site by the communists and gypsies. It was a perfect place to hide his treasures.

Apart from his golden eagle, Luis had misappropriated money and artefacts from the various offices he had worked in. He would falsify books of account, then apprehend the bookkeeper who he would usually force to confess and commit suicide in his cell, filled with remorse, and no doubt assisted on his last journey by Luis himself. The authorities recovered none of these funds. They lay beneath the Convent of the Blessed Saints, close to Madrid. After dark, Luis arrived to collect his booty.

He planned to stay in France and dispose of the golden eagle there, while doing his job with the Gestapo. He was sure occupied Paris would provide plenty of opportunities for a man of his talents. With his proceeds safely and anonymously banked in Switzerland, he would retire to that secure country, or maybe somewhere in South America, to live out his days in absolute luxury.

He took a canvas bag and a powerful flashlight from the trunk of the car and entered the crypt. It smelt of dried, long mummified corpses, overlaid by a sweet but putrid odour. Six or seven desiccated bodies lay on benches around the walls. An eighth corpse was quite recent and the foetid smell came from that corner of the crypt. At first, the smell of death did not bother the *coronel*, for he had seen and caused more death than most men, but he felt that there was something more here, not a smell, but an unsettling aura in the vault, a sense of great foreboding, a malignant feeling. It was as though a cold sliver of fear had penetrated his brain.

He shook his head and laughed at himself. *Well*, he thought, *it is a morbid place, and, in the middle of the night, bound to seem more so.*

He went to the rear wall and removed the stone prayer tablets that hid the entrance to the tunnel. He was about to enter when he noticed something different about the latest occupant. The shroud seemed to be disturbed. Trying to ignore a rising tide of disquiet, he approached the corpse, the binding shroud torn, shreds of it hanging down from the burial platform. He felt relieved and grinned at his own stupidity. Of course, rats! There must be rats around here; they had disturbed the corpse!

He could not resist a closer look. As he shone the light on the body, he saw that something ripped the shroud into long shreds about the head of the deceased. That was strange; rats would not tear it like that, they would gnaw holes in it. He moved closer, recoiling in horror, dropping the flashlight; it rolled away, leaving him in darkness. He felt his heart almost stop and his mind reel from what he had seen. Retrieving the torch, he waited until his heart stopped racing and his breathing eased before taking a closer look. Something had ripped the partly desiccated flesh in strips from the cheeks and forehead of the body; its eyes were missing, the nose torn. He could not believe it, but he knew what he was seeing. As a young man, he had friends who indulged in the sport of falconry; he had seen the rabbits they had caught and how the predator birds fed. He was looking at a similar thing.

So that was it! A bird had gotten in and done the damage. Once more, he chided himself for being a fool. He paused; it was a well-sealed vault; no bird could get in here. Besides, he had seen nests and chicken coops and pigeon lofts. Birds were not tidy animals. They left behind their faeces, feathers, roosting marks and the remains of their prey. The crypt was clear of such trash. *Madre de Dios*. He breathed. *What is going on here?* It was certainly strange, but he forced all thoughts of the terror he felt to one side and quickly entered the tunnel. He must recover his booty and get out of this place before he went insane! It was a short distance from the cellar. Here the air was fresher, and he quickly forgot his sense of doom.

When he entered, he quickly scooped up the banknotes he had left there, along with some of the more valuable jewellery – with the statue, he could carry no more on his journey. All this he placed in the canvas bag before turning to the golden eagle. *That was strange*, he thought. *I am sure I wrapped it up securely when I left it here!* The steel container lay open, the oilskin wrapping was loose, and he could see the eagle's head partly protruding from it, one emerald eye gleaming in the torchlight.

It seemed to project a self-satisfied look at him, and there were some dark marks around the beak of the bird. He felt the ice creeping up his spine once more and the terror roiling in his gut. His heart rate rose alarmingly, and his breathing became ragged and shallow. *Stop it! Stop it! You will go mad! Get out of here!* He snatched up the statue and his bag and ran down the tunnel and out into the night. As he fled, his feet disturbed some feathers on the floor. They rose and fluttered back down again; he did not see them. Outside, as the cool night air dried the sweat from his brow, he felt his heart and head return to normal.

*Engañar! Fool! Pull yourself together hombre! There are no ghosts.* He rested awhile, sitting on a gravestone, gradually regaining his composure. Finally, he rose and walked to the car. He picked up the statue of the eagle. *I will clean it,* he decided, *and I will take a good look at it. It will be the last I will see of it until I reach Paris.* Taking his handkerchief from a pocket, he rubbed the statue. The marks on the beak drew his attention. They were brown. If he had not known better, he could have sworn that he looked at dried blood stains. *What a stupid fool you are,* he laughed. *How could that be?* Luis dared not think about the torn flesh of the corpse. He wrapped the statue in its oilskin. He tried not to look at the eyes shining in the bright moonlight, but they involuntarily drew his eyes to them. *¡Dios!* They were moving! They cast a look of deadly malevolence towards him; he dragged his eyes away and quickly wrapped it tightly, binding it with a canvas strap. He must be hallucinating!

Luis drove back to Madrid, his mind a turmoil of conflicting emotions. His common sense told him that nothing had happened, but images of the bird's eyes kept intruding. That night he dreamed of rotting flesh. He heard the keening shrieks of eagles; he saw those emerald eyes darting everywhere. Mixed with those images, he saw the faces of the hundreds he had killed, tortured and raped. He could hear their screams, particularly those of the women.

## Madrid, Spain, 1940

He woke, sweat-stained and trembling, the terrors of his nightmare still nibbling at his consciousness. After coffee and some breakfast, he dressed in street clothes and drove the car back to its owner.

He spent his last day closing his office and assigning his files to his replacement, *Coronel* Pedro Alaró. Alaró was an appropriate choice; he was a brutal and dissolute animal of a man who wielded his authority without mercy or remorse. Almost everybody hated him, but none dared to stand up to him. After a day's reading of the files together, Luis was ready to hand over to the new commander.

He looked drawn and pale, not the bluff and hearty bull of a man known as The Black Death. He was having the dream now with increasing frequency and had slept badly; some nights he had not slept at all, forcing himself to remain awake for fear the dream would return.

He had taken to drinking heavily to numb his senses and drive out the dream, but with only limited success. He could hardly wait to begin his journey north. Luis was sure he would recover his equilibrium in his new posting. He dared not open the oilskin wrapping or look at those emerald eyes.

Across the desk, Pedro Alaró evaluated the man he was going to replace. To him, Luis looked in terrible shape, drawn, with pouches under his eyes, baggy clothes testifying to recent weight loss. The arrogant look had disappeared. *You have had enough of it*, he surmised. *Perhaps you will be better off out of it.* He had been told that Luis was due for a promotion and a staff job soon. In the meantime, he would be on leave. *Good*, mused Pedro. *Maybe you need a rest, amigo.* He said, '*Coronel* Escardo, perhaps you would like a last tour of the building while I explain some extra measures I intend to introduce. I would be pleased to have your approval.'

They spent some hours on their inspection. Luis found the extra measures planned by Pedro to be harsher than the current ones. Suddenly, the barbaric nature of his work elbowed its way into the remnants of his conscience, and he felt nauseous and light-headed. *It will please me to be out of this hell*, he thought.

They had reached the cells in the basement. There were many prisoners, young and old, male and female, even a battered-looking priest. Somewhere, Luis could hear the thuds and groans as some unfortunates were 'interviewed', and the occasional piercing female scream. 'The guards are having some fun,' Pedro remarked.

They came across a young woman alone in a cell. She was filthy, her hair a rat's nest, bruises on all her visible flesh; blood ran down her thighs, raped multiple times. She had a crazed look in her eyes. As they approached, she screamed, '¡*Dios mío! el muerte negro!* He is here, God save us! Have mercy on us!'

In his fragile state, Luis was unprepared for this. 'Who is this woman?' he demanded.

'She is a communist, and her village priest has sworn that she is a witch, possessed by the devil. She has confessed, although it took several days. The men had an awfully long visit to her *coño*! Many had to return three times.' Pedro snickered. 'They said she was very good and struggled fiercely, much to their delight!'

The prisoner looked at Luis and extended a trembling finger in his direction. 'I curse you, *Coronel*,' she said to Luis. 'I curse you for your crimes, for the hundreds you have violated and tortured. You will not live much longer. You will die in agony. Your body will rot from the outside and shed its parts like a bird moulting until it can no longer support your vile spirit. You will burn in Hell forever!' She collapsed, sobbing, to the concrete floor.

Luis jokingly passed it off as the ravings of the demented. Many had cursed him before, and he remained unharmed. But he felt a brief spike of fear twist in his guts, and he was quick to end his visit.

Early the next evening, under the cover of darkness, armed with his papers and several identities, he drove across a remote part of the border where two Germans waited to greet him.

# DEATH IN PARIS

*Embassy of Spain, Paris, France, 1940*

Luis had made a long train journey to the city. After the Germans met him, they indicated he should enter the car they had waiting. Neither of them wore a uniform. They offered no greetings and asked no questions. They drove him in silence to the railway station in Perpignan, where a train was to leave shortly for Paris.

It was a long journey to the French capital, but Luis had a sleeping compartment to himself in a first-class car. Tired after the last few weeks, he slept for most of the way, noting with satisfaction that his sleep was untroubled by his nightmare. Could such a thing as a simple change of scenery do this? Perhaps the prospect of a new task had removed the burdens of the old.

As instructed, he made his way to the Spanish embassy, where a military attaché who showed him to his accommodation met him and arranged for an official meeting that evening. *Capitán de Navío* Ernesto de Mercinda met Luis in his office at eight o'clock that night.

'Welcome, *Coronel*,' he said. 'You have been fortunate to be posted here to one of the great cities of the Third Reich. You will have the right connections here; Reichsführer-SS Himmler himself authorised your recruitment to the Gestapo cause. They expect that there will be more resistance to German occupation as the war continues. Already, they have looted all the food from the countryside and the peasants are hungry; that will only get worse. The new laws regarding *los Judios* have antagonised non-Jews. The French are pragmatic enough to realise that many of their doctors, entrepreneurs, scientists and artisans are Jewish. They want them left alone to play a part in the new economy. They cannot see the wisdom in getting rid of such talent. However, the Germans seem determined to transport large numbers to the camps. They will need you to organise contacts and methods with which to control the malcontents, especially those who can begin an armed resistance. I know how successful you were in Spain. I am sure you will continue in that vein. Meanwhile, enjoy the pleasures Paris offers. You will find fine wine and food still up there with the world's best since the Germans keep all that for themselves, and the women, *Mi Dios, las mujeres*, they are ever willing. You will have such fun! In the morning, the Gestapo will send a car for you. Enjoy yourself. *Buenos noches.*'

## Gestapo Headquarters, 11 rue de Saussaies, Paris, France, 1940

*Kriminalinspektor* Walter Bormann was looking forward to meeting the man from Madrid. His job could become much easier with a new set of ideas and an experienced man to help with the legwork. They forced him to depend on the French police. The flics were lazy and incompetent, and he had his doubts about their loyalty to the new Vichy regime. They needed a fresh approach.

Luis was travelling under a false name. The Germans knew this, but they did not need to know his proper name. The highest level in Berlin had recruited him; that was all they needed to know; to know more might be dangerous. He used the code name 'Max', German enough, cosmopolitan enough, and common enough to be inconspicuous.

He left the Embassy and took an apartment in the Avenue Martinique, where he established the image of a rich playboy. He had access to the highest circles of government and the occupying powers, and he spent considerable time cultivating contacts and soliciting information. Some women were the best talkers when their clothes were off, and they writhed in their passion. Despite his rapacious preferences, he could play the gentle and accomplished lover when necessary. More than a dozen of these women found themselves in the cells of 11 *rue de Saussaies* because of careless talk.

He taught the Gestapo some of his techniques. Luis had found the guilty to be most susceptible to threats rather than physical abuse, although he remained ever ready to employ it. He offered them and their families a brutal treatment if they refused to cooperate. Threatening their children with rape was his favourite technique, and it seldom failed. When it did, he brought the children to the cells where he made the parents watch as a group of his most bestial men carried out his threat. He had long ago learned that you do not threaten unless you mean to carry through with it.

He planned to sell the golden eagle as soon as he could. The Swiss border was still open to him, but he could not carry the eagle through the border controls. He planned to send his money there when he had completed the sale. He had compiled a list of dealers in gold and precious stones and began making general enquiries as to the value of his statue. When he described the enormous emerald to them, they universally disbelieved him. Emeralds that size were the stuff of greatly magnified dreams, he was told, but he had more luck in determining the value of the gold. He had weighed the statue, although he did not dare to open the parcel. Allowing for the stones and the oilskin, he found he had around five kilograms of gold. It was numbing. At the present price of gold, he had around one hundred and ninety thousand dollars.

It was astounding, but how was he to sell it? Its value as an artefact would be much higher, and he did not want to melt it down. No single purchaser could buy it, certainly in wartime Paris. And how much would the emeralds be worth? He did not know what to do.

One evening he brought Michelle, his current paramour, to his apartment. He never disguised that his only interest in these girls was sex, and so it was not long before they were in the bedroom, disrobing, kissing and fondling. He led her to the bed, but she gave a little gasp of dismay as he drew down the coverlet. There on the sheets were hundreds of dark hairs; they could only have been his! He looked again. There was no doubt of it. Michelle went to the bathroom and returned with a hairbrush choked with the same dark hair. She ran it across his head, whereupon large tufts of his hair pulled out. It was awful!

She looked at him in disgust. 'I will go now,' she said. 'You may not see me for a while. I have to visit relatives in Rheims.' She hurriedly dressed and made for the door.

The incident dumbfounded 'Max'. What was happening to him? He ran a bath and climbed in; perhaps he needed a good soaking to rid himself of whatever was causing the problem. He moved the washcloth over his chest. Great God! Patches of his chest hair came out! He tried his leg with the same result. Luis looked again and saw that his pubic hair had become very thin. He could see patches of his skin through the thatch.

'Max' scrambled from the bath. Too frightened to towel himself off, he gently patted his body with the towel, trying hard not to dislodge any more hair. He moved to the living room and opened a bottle of dark red wine. Halfway through the bottle, he remembered the woman in the cells in Madrid, the mad one, the witch! Could she have really cursed him? 'Come,' he said aloud. 'That is arrant nonsense, fairy stories. Forget it!' He finished the wine and went to bed.

In the morning, he found he had lost no more hair overnight. He cancelled his appointments and sought a doctor. The medico had no explanation. 'You may have a nervous dermatitis; your sudden change of climate has brought it on, or perhaps it is nervous in nature. Have you been having any such episodes, hallucinations or fits or the like? Are you afraid of something?'

'Max' did not want to disclose such matters to anyone, least of all someone unknown to him. 'No,' he said. 'It only just started, and now it has stopped.' He tugged at his forelock, which remained firmly anchored to his head. The hair loss did not reappear. 'Max', however, was eager to do something about the statue. He had a tiny stirring in his brain. Could the eagle carry a curse? He imagined again the moving eyes, the malevolent gaze. No, no; such ideas were madness. Nevertheless, the sooner he could turn it into money, the happier he would be.

That night he had his dream again, filled with the screams of large birds, the cries of his victims, chief among them the commissar he had ordered raped to death. The emerald eyes bored into him; they appeared to grow larger. The bird opened his beak and screamed again. Blood smeared its beak, and strips of flesh hung from it. He awoke, sweating, in a senseless terror, a black despair. Something convinced him that the sooner he could sell the statue, the better it would be. In the morning, his bed was littered with hair, and among it was the unmistakable sight of a feather! He thought he was losing his mind. He avoided sleep, to cease washing for fear he would scrub off more hair.

Eventually, he shaved his head so that the hair loss was not so clear. There were some small red sores on his forearms. Now he felt the dread of the woman's curse. It terrified him. At his work, his companions had noticed his tiredness, his sunken eyes and his weight loss. He avoided it for some time, but eventually had to disclose his problem to the chief of the Gestapo in the city, Konrad Schultz.

Schultz was a confidante of Goering and Himmler. 'Max' knew of the organised looting of treasure all over occupied Europe. He knew that vast quantities of paintings, bullion, jewellery and works of art were being shipped to vaults in Switzerland, vaults of the tight-lipped and avaricious bankers. Luis had seen the convoys of SS trucks, tightly sealed, and escorted by heavily armed troops, stream from the city. He knew the Nazis wanted all the treasure they could get, and he wondered if he could make a deal with them. He invited Schultz to dinner at an exclusive restaurant, one reserved for the Nazis and their camp followers, including prominent officials of the Vichy government. Luis did not tell Schultz the full story, merely that he had a fabulous piece of art he wanted to sell. Perhaps the good chief could help him? There would be a generous commission, of course.

'I will see what I can do,' he said. 'Say nothing about this until you hear from me.'

In the morning, 'Max' found more hair in his bed and more sores on his body. They were now on his legs, stomach and back. The ones on his forearms had started to weep. He treated them with some antiseptic lotion and bound them up. He was desperate to hear from Schultz. A week later, Schultz telephoned him. 'You are in luck,' he said. *'Der Reichsführer-SS* Himmler himself will be in Paris next week. He is most anxious to talk to you. Tuesday at nine in the morning, in my office.'

Although it was only days away, 'Max' felt he had been waiting for months by the time they ushered him into Schultz's office. He passed through a perimeter of grim-looking *SS* troops, was thoroughly searched down to his body cavities, and had to surrender his pistol before they granted him the privilege of the audience with Himmler.

*Der Reichsführer-SS* was in a good mood this morning, and he greeted 'Max' with warmth and a Nazi salute. 'Max' looked at his unprepossessing figure, at the wire-rimmed glasses, at the weak, almost non-existent chin and the weasel eyes. How could such a creature rise to such a lofty position?

Himmler, however, was quick, intelligent and to the point. He asked many questions. 'Max' was vague about the statue, but Himmler would have none of it. They forced him to disclose the details. *'Mein Herr,'* he said, 'You cannot expect to recoup the full value of such a thing. Bring it to me this afternoon. I will have my people examine it and put a value on it. Let us hope you are not wasting my time.'

Later in the day, 'Max' returned to the office, carrying the oilskin package. They had ordered the guards to admit him immediately and not to examine his package. In the office, he unwrapped the statue and placed it on the desk. Both the Germans gave sharp intakes of breath at the sight of it. *'Wunderschön!'* exclaimed *Der Reichsführer-SS*. 'It is a most impressive piece, but I am afraid it is not worth much to the Reich. We cannot sell it, at least until the end of the war. Do you have a figure in mind?'

'Max' did not know what to say. He knew the Germans could appropriate it now without compensation. He had only his connection to Franco to prevent that, and it appeared that Hitler had lost interest in enticing Spain into the war on his side. 'It is worth about two hundred thousand US dollars for the gold alone. Truly, it must be worth much more as a collectible, but I am eager to realise its value. I will listen to any offer you care to make.'

Himmler had disguised the raw avarice in his eyes. *Mein Gott*, he thought, *he is right. It could be worth a million.* It would shore up the *Reich* in its time of need, underwriting the purchase of iron ore, rubber, oil and a multitude of precious metals such as manganese, tungsten and aluminium. Moreover, he knew that fat fool Goering would do anything to gain such a treasure. If he could get it, and present it to *der Führer*, he could get anything from him, anything! That would be one in the eye for Goering!

He turned to the Spaniard. '*Der Reich* can offer you one hundred thousand for it, no more. I remind you I could just take it now and give you nothing. I am afraid that when you deal with the devil, you must make the best of any offer you get.'

That shocked 'Max', but he hid it. *You hijo de puta*, he thought, *lobos del diablo. No doubt I will see you in hell.* But he reasoned he should quit while he was in front. He desperately needed to be rid of the statue. He wanted the money and one hundred thousand dollars was more than he had ever dreamed of possessing. Reluctantly, he agreed. The money would go to the bank account he had opened in Zurich before he would hand over the statue.

'*Nein*, you will leave it here, so I know it will be safe. I cannot risk losing it now.' 'Max' looked at the statue. The eyes swivelled to look at him. You fool, they seemed to say, you fool. He looked away.

When he had ushered the man from the office, Schultz, who had remained speechless throughout the whole affair, smiled at his master. '*Unglaublich*,' he said, 'incredible. *Der Führer* will be well pleased with you.'

'And with you, my dear Schultz. I will take charge of the statue; you will come to Berlin in a week. I am sure *Der Führer* will want to thank you personally for the splendid work you have done for the Reich.'

'And the money …'

'We will pay it. However, you must say nothing of this. We do not want to upset our friends in Madrid. Franco may not know of this. *Der Führer* may want his help soon against our greatest enemy. *Heil Hitler!*'

Himmler was pleased. He would tell the others he had paid two hundred. Himmler would pocket one hundred thousand. He planned how he would return the item to Berlin. The plane was too vulnerable; the RAF often sent fighters to France on lightning raids. He was sure that the Luftwaffe would protect them, but it was too big a risk. He would secrete the statue somewhere in Paris and consult his friends about the best way to transport it. An armoured train came to mind.

## Avenue Martinique, Paris, 1940

Luis went home to his apartment. He had mixed feelings. He had virtually given away his treasure, but he reasoned he had gained it by a stroke of good luck and a homicidal impulse. In any event, he would have more money than he had ever seen before. He decided to celebrate his good fortune.

He telephoned Paulette; Michelle had vanished without a trace. Paulette was reluctant; she had heard of his brutality in the prison, but the Gestapo were paying her well to service these men. After they had dined, they returned to the apartment. Although he craved sex as much as usual, he had not been performing well of late. He felt tired, sick and full of the horrors of his dreams. He reached a climax and satisfied the girl, but he wanted her out of his apartment as soon as possible. His breathing had barely returned to normal before he was urging her to dress and go. She complained at his rebuff and threw aside the covers. '*Merde!*' she exclaimed. 'I have the damned curse!' Blood covered the sheets.

Paulette went to the bathroom to clean herself, only to find she was not menstruating at all. It was a relief because she knew when she was due and feared something had gone wrong, but why the blood? She returned to the bedroom and pulled up short, emitting a small shriek. '*Mon Dieu*, what has happened, *chèrie?*'

The sheet was a crazy pattern of blood streaks and black hair; amid it was Luis, pale and looking dumbfounded. He was gibbering, 'The witch, the witch,' repeatedly. His eyes swung desperately around the room. 'The eagle, the eagle,' he cried. Paulette took another look and bolted.

Some hours later, Luis staggered from the bed and went to the bathroom. He just had to clean himself. He lay in the bath and watched as every hair on his body washed away under the cloth. The sores were now all weeping, bleeding into the water. He rose, dried himself, and went out to find a taxi. He went to the nearest hospital, where the shocked staff admitted him and placed him in a tepid bath. His skin was still weeping, and no one knew what to do. Eventually, a doctor saw him. Doctor Charles Pironne had never seen such an affliction. He retired to the hospital library, where he read long into the night.

In the ward, Luis was in a drug-induced sleep. His wounds ached and throbbed. He could not bear contact with the sheets. In his coma, the dream returned. An eagle screamed. The victims looked at him, but now they were smiling, not in welcome, but in jubilation at his demise. The much-violated commissar was there, as well as the soldier he had killed for the statue. Emerald eyes cut through him with a look of such malevolence that he felt his soul quail. He tried to mutter prayers, but the words came out all garbled.

Finally, the woman from the cells in Madrid appeared, pointing at him. In a moment of lucidity, he could hear her voice: 'Your body will rot … and shed its parts like a bird moulting … your vile spirit … vile spirit … vile spirit …' In the morning he awoke, his mind lucid, to find the doctor looking at him.

'You have caused us some concern, my friend,' he said, 'but I think I have stumbled upon something that might explain your condition. Ancient apothecaries have described your symptoms before in the sixteenth century. For a period of years, a sizable number of patients, all male, presented similarly. There was speculation about gypsies and witchcraft and curses, but none of this proved true. The curious thing is that almost all these men were from Hungary and Romania, where there are large numbers of gypsies. Did someone curse you?'

Luis looked at his body. Many of his sores had disappeared, others looked as if they were healing. He felt much better. The pain had gone. 'Don't be silly,' he said. He discharged himself and took a taxi to return to his apartment. About halfway there, he felt an itch on his stomach. Without looking, he raised his shirt and scratched. It felt strange to his touch.

Luis looked down at his midriff; he had torn strips of his skin away, exposing the yellow fatty tissue. He almost cried out. The taxi drew up to his address, and he stepped out. Blood covered the front of his shirt, but the driver seemed not to notice. As he moved to his door, he heard the cry of an eagle. Looking around, he saw the bird perched in a nearby tree, its eyes fixed upon him. Suddenly it seemed that the eagle had turned to gold, and its eyes glowed with a green fire. He screamed and rushed into his apartment. When he looked out his window, the bird had gone.

'I am not mad,' he cried, 'I am not!' The sun must have gilded the bird momentarily, and he had imagined the eyes, surely.

He opened a bottle of wine, but it did nothing for him. He reached for the brandy. Finally, he went to his bed. The dream returned, and it woke him in a lather of sweat. The pain had returned; an itch had returned; it was torment. He tried to scratch his stomach again, but his nails tore more flesh from his torso, He could see the gleam of an exposed rib. Luis tried to get out of the bed, but when he stood up, his ankle buckled. He lay on the floor and felt for the ankle – the flesh had gone! All that held the foot to his leg were the ligaments!

He could not speak. He struggled into a sitting position and looked at his stomach. As he watched, the minor cut he had scratched bulged like a door being forced from within.

Luis saw the glistening coils of his intestines pushing out into his lap. He looked out the window at the dark night. He could see the shadow of an eagle cross the face of the moon, and he was falling into the dark void of unconsciousness and death. The last thing he saw was the soundless, gaping mouth of the screaming commissar.

## Die Miners Bank aus Zürich, Switzerland 1940

Gustav Weissmann had never seen the owner of account F-258774196; the client had made all his arrangements by telephone and returned the signed documents from Paris by mail. Today, authorisation from the Reichsbank had transferred one hundred thousand dollars to the account in Berlin. Gustav had seen many such transfers. They had come from Poland, Denmark and Norway, from Germany, Luxembourg and Belgium. He did not know who the parties were, but his incisive mind soon saw that the funds always involved countries under the German occupation.

He did not know it, but the money would remain in Account F-258774196, untouched until the year 2011, when new laws facilitated the return of the plunder seized by the Nazis to its rightful owners. This money went into consolidated revenue since they could identify no owner. In fact, he would never know it. Gustav Weissmann went to his heavenly reward in 1998.

## Hauptbahnhof, Berlin

*Reichskriminaldirektor* Konrad Schultz stepped from the train in Berlin and looked around for his promised car and driver. He had splashed out on a new suit for the occasion. He had found a good tailoring house in Paris, Juden of course, and he promised them protection in return for free suits. *This was a particularly good one,* he thought.

Two Gestapo men appeared at the end of the platform. Several SS soldiers armed with machine pistols accompanied them, and they strode purposefully towards him. He smiled; they were laying it on for him, no doubt.

He wondered if he would meet *der Führer* personally. The leading man halted. 'Schultz?' he said. 'You will accompany me to Gestapo headquarters. Please hand over your pistol.'

'Of course,' said Schultz, 'but why my pistol?'

'Because you are under arrest *Dummkopf*, by order of *Der Reichsführer-SS* on charges of corruption and theft of State property.' He was still protesting his innocence the next morning as they led him to the firing squad.

# AN UNLUCKY BIRD

*SS Headquarters, Prinz Albrechtstrasse 108, Berlin, 1940*

*Der Reichsführer-SS* was in a quandry. He wanted to go back to Paris himself to retrieve the golden eagle, but he was under intense pressure to remain in Berlin. The battle for the skies over England was entering its last stages and Germany had not done well.

Goering had promised to eliminate the RAF in a matter of days. However, the RAF had other ideas, shooting down almost two-thirds of the aircraft sent to destroy it, and now had total control of English airspace. With operation *Seelöwe*, the invasion of Britain, cancelled, Hitler looked to the east, to the vast territories of the Soviet Union. For the moment, he had lost interest in the British and the planning for operation *Barbarossa*, the invasion of Russia, was ramping up. The leaders of the Reich were too busy for visits to Paris. *Der Reichsführer-SS* decided he must send someone he trusted implicitly for the task. He usually found that the people he had some hold over made the most trustworthy envoys. Even better if they held high rank and were ardent Nazis.

He calculated for a while before asking his secretary to fetch several personnel files for him. He read them assiduously. Finally, he reached a decision. He made some phone calls before issuing an order to bring *Standartenführer* Erich Borden to his office at nine o'clock the next morning.

### Winestrasse 237, Berlin, 1940

At that very moment, the good *Standartenführer* was lying in bed with the wife of a subordinate officer whom he had sent to tour the cities of Poland, winkling out Jews for extermination. This was a tiring and emotional business, for the great gas chambers were yet to be constructed and these *drecksjuden* had to be shot individually and buried. Borden worried about the effects this was having on his troops. It was incredibly stressful for them.

He rolled over and stroked the generous breasts of his companion once more. Soon she was ready again, and their lovemaking was frantic. *Poor Hans*, he thought, *this woman is far too much for him. I am doing him a favour, in fact, bearing some of his load.* The woman moaned once more and reached for him. 'Again,' she said, 'I cannot get enough of it. Put it in me again!'

He lay spent, losing interest in her vulgar, selfish lovemaking. Besides, he was late for the office. He pushed her aside roughly. 'It is time to be gone, *Liebling*,' he said. 'I have work to do.' He dressed hurriedly and left her apartment. '*Mein Gott*,' he exclaimed, 'she is like a bitch in heat. No one could satisfy her!'

Hans never had that chance. Partisans ambushed him a week later, but she had no difficulty finding a replacement. In 1943, she perished in a seedy hotel room in Hamburg in the arms of a drunken U-Boat officer, as bombs rained down. She had been reluctant to leave her bed for an air raid shelter. Nobody missed her.

### SS Headquarters, Prinz Albrechtstrasse 108, Berlin, 1940

When Erich reached his office and received the summons from the *Reichsführer*, he experienced a whirlwind of emotions. Was he in trouble, had someone denounced him? What could this mean? Even men of his rank (equivalent to colonel) feared the vicious Himmler, who never forgot one's mistakes, and who revelled in handing out humiliating or fatal punishments. He made sure he dressed perfectly before the meeting. He had racked his brains but could not think of anything that would have incurred the *Reichsführer's* wrath. So, it was with confidence that he entered the hallowed chamber.

Himmler was in good spirits this morning. He watched as Borden snapped an immaculate Nazi salute. 'Sit down, *Standartenführer*, I have a grave and secret task for you. The future of our Reich may depend on how well you do this. Here is what you are to do …'

The *Reichsführer* laid out the task before him. He was to go to Paris, retrieve a steel container, and bring it back to Berlin. He was to travel by special train and ordered not to open the box. To confuse others, he would have orders to undertake a review of all the SS and Gestapo units operating out of 11 *rue de Saussaies*. This would give him a legitimate cover and ensure that the SS in Paris would be in deadly fear of him. He would have no trouble with them, for he was to carry a letter from the *Reichsführer* himself requesting full cooperation on this important task. *This is good*, he mused. *I will have to spend at least a week in the city;* he looked forward to the fine dining and the fashionable women he would have. All, in all, a satisfactory assignment. Himmler looked at him shrewdly. 'You must not fail in this task. It is of vital importance. Go now, you leave tonight.'

Borden clicked his heels and delivered a salute. '*Heil Hitler!* You may depend on me. I would gladly give my life to the Reich but of course, you know that already, *Herr Reichsführer.*' He marched to the door.

He had it half opened when Himmler spoke. '*Ja, Standartenführer,* and I also know about *Winestrasse 237*. Be careful, *Standartenführer,* very careful indeed.' Borden felt an icy chill run down his spine.

### Le Club Chapeau Noir, Paris, 1940

The Black Hat club was at the apex of Parisienne nightlife. When the Germans came, the proprietor was happy to welcome them, another million or more extra clients. Unlike many upmarket establishments, they did not set aside the Black Hat for the exclusive use of the occupiers. The proprietor was a member of the far right and supported the Vichy government; he would have been happier for France to join with Germany and fight the communists together. They would have to eventually, he argued.

The premises teemed with high-ranking German officers, Vichy officials, and those whom the war had enriched, chiefly the pimps and black marketeers. News reporters and diplomats from the US and other embassies also flocked there. For anyone who wanted to know where the wind blew, or more importantly, where it was about to blow, it was an essential venue.

### Maurice and Louise – The Pleasure Dome

Maurice Benin was a pimp. There was no other way to describe him. It would have insulted him if he knew he was thought of as such, for that was not how he viewed himself. He was a native of Paris, born in the affluent suburb of Passy in the 16e *arrondissement*, his family moderately wealthy, his father a consulting gynaecologist to the rich and famous. Maybe that is why he developed an obsession with female genitalia and sexual adventure from an early age.

They had dismissed him from two schools and his first and only job for engaging in illicit sexual behaviour. He would boast that he had lost his virginity at age thirteen and had spent the rest of his life looking for it in the *vagins* of half of the women in Paris. Therefore, it was no surprise to find him in *Le Club Chapeau Noir* with an impressive stable of young women who commanded higher prices than any whore in Europe.

His big break had come in 1935 when his father died, leaving him a large estate. He no longer had to seduce young women; he just went out and purchased them. This got him thinking about the cost of his favourite commodity and how many francs he spent to satisfy his gargantuan appetite. It would make sense, he reasoned, to be collecting the money, not spending it.

There was a beautiful woman called Louise who worked in a

bordello near the Tour Eiffel and whose affection he had purchased several times. She seemed genuine in her feelings towards him, so one evening he made her a proposition. Would she not work for him? Together they could make a lot of money. Demand was beyond the industry's capacity to supply. She would, and she became his live-in lover. She did not mind if he had other women; sometimes she even joined them in a *ménage à trois*. He had discovered that rare but precious commodity, a woman who truly and unreservedly enjoyed sex.

They rented a large house and turned it into a residence for themselves and a training school for young ladies. Louise recruited them; Maurice introduced them to pleasures they had not dreamed possible. Soon they had twenty girls in their employ, as well as security men, hairdressers, beauticians, medical people and couturiers. They always kept their girls impeccably dressed, well-mannered, free of disease and they had no equals in the art of lovemaking. Of course, the fees they charged were off the scale, but there was no shortage of men prepared to pay, and soon they became very wealthy.

After a brief conversation with Louise and a couple of her friends, both wealthy married ladies, they began a service for women, staffed by handsome young lotharios. To Maurice's surprise, they were as much in demand as the pretty ladies were. They had plans for similar services for homosexuals of both genders, but when the Germans came, they thought it wiser to put such ideas into cold storage for the time being.

## The Corruption of Standartenführer Erich Borden

*Standartenführer* Borden was enjoying his time in Paris. He had imposed his authority immediately, discovering two young officers stealing from the office funds. Only a few francs, but it was enough to throw Borden into a righteous fury. He ordered them to be stripped of their commissions, reduced to the lowest rank and sent to Berlin, where they would endure a year in prison before being posted to a punishment battalion. There was no more trouble. He had the run of the headquarters. Retrieving the package would be easy.

Erich Borden first went to the Black Hat at the suggestion of some of his brother officers. 'Mind you take plenty of money,' they joked, '*les femmes sont chers!*' They were indeed expensive, but the performance was delightful. On his second visit, he enjoyed the company of Noni, a dark beauty whose eyes were mysterious and deep. As he undressed her, he marvelled at her perfect body. He had never had a woman as beautiful as this! She taught him things even he did not know; her body became an instrument of passion, and he played it with considerable skill until spent. Lying with her, he felt as he had not done before. Was he finally in love? He knew that forbidden, but on subsequent nights he went only to her. She responded as if she too thought there was much more than a commercial nature to their couplings.

As his week in the city ended, he found that the idea of returning to Germany without her was anathema. He was desperate in his need of her. Erich thought of nothing, day and night, but her long silky legs, the perfect globes of her breasts, the sweet symmetry of her sex. He must have her forever. The thought of other men possessing her would drive him mad! When he expressed his feelings, Noni sat on the edge of the bed and wept. 'Erich, I love you also, but it cannot be. I am what I am, and you are a senior officer. You would ruin your career. They would probably send you to the front. If only we were rich, we could flee to Switzerland. We could be happy there.'

He agonised all night. He could not sleep. In the early morning, his mind returned to the box Himmler had sent him for. What was in it? Whatever it *was*, it must be valuable. This might be my chance to be rich and have Noni as well. Do I have the guts to do it? He knew failure would bring death in a most exquisite form to them both. They would probably take her to a punishment battalion of half-crazed men and make him watch as they raped her. Nevertheless, he knew he must take this chance.

## *Gestapo Headquarters, 11 rue de Saussaies, Paris, France, 1940*

Erich arrived at the Gestapo building just at curfew time. There would be fewer people on the streets to see him at that time. The guards did not question him, for the SS worked all day and night on their gruesome tasks throughout the city.

He climbed to the third floor, where there was an access ladder to a storage area inside the floor space. He carried the ladder to the door of the compartment. It had the look of long abandonment about it. When he opened the trapdoor, it subjected him to a torrent of dust, rat droppings and dead cockroaches. *Good*, he thought, *no one has been here for some time.* He levered his head and shoulders inside and flashed his torch around. He saw nothing but boxes of long-forgotten files, broken typewriters and rags. '*Scheiß!*' he said. He was looking for a metal box, painted grey and emblazoned with the eagle and swastika emblem of the Reich.

There was nothing like it in sight. He would have to climb right into the cavity and move some boxes. The third box looked like all the others, but when he tried to move it, he could feel its heavy weight. Himmler had concealed his box inside another. Erich struggled down the ladder with the box and closed the hatch. He would have to clean the detritus from himself and the floor, so he went looking for a cleaner's cupboard. He found one nearby and cleaned up his mess before bending to pick up the steel box. It was very heavy; no wonder he had difficulty negotiating the ladder, for he needed both hands to carry it.

*Mien Gott*, but it was heavy, all right! He could just lift it by one handle so that it looked like a briefcase but could not carry it for long that way. Finally, he picked it up two-handed and staggered down the stairs to a side door that led to the motor pool. He had a car and driver allocated to him, but he had long since dismissed him for the night. He had not imagined the box would be so heavy; to carry it through the streets would be impossible. He left it just outside the door and went to find a vehicle.

There were about a dozen vehicles in the yard, trucks, staff cars, even an ambulance. He found what he was looking for down the back of the yard, a BMW motorbike and sidecar. He scuttled back to the door and carried the box to the machine, placing it in the sidecar under its cover. He swung himself into the seat.

Thankfully, this machine was for field use, and that meant there was no ignition lock and key. He simply turned the knurled ignition switch and kicked the starter. The bike responded immediately, and he headed towards the street. There was a sentry in a dimly lit hut at the street front and a striped barrier that was closed. *Gott im Himmel!* He would have to stop. The guard was a smartly turned-out *SS-Rottenführer*, armed with a machine pistol.

He looked at Erich with hard eyes that showed no respect for Erich's officer status. '*Heil Hitler,*' he said. 'You cannot take out that bike tonight, sir. The guard commander has ordered that no vehicles leave tonight. There is a senior officer who will inspect them in the morning. We cannot use them tonight.'

Erich was almost struck dumb; then he remembered. *He* was the senior officer. *He* had ordered this vehicle inspection himself. Erich cursed himself for a *Dummkopf*. Erich would have to show Himmler's letter to this man! But wait, even if he allowed the bike to leave, there would be a paper trail, a name, a time. That would pin him down precisely in the event of an enquiry, and there would be one hell of an enquiry if Himmler's box went missing! There was only one thing he could do now. He dismounted and moved into the dim circle of light from the hut. The sentry stiffened a little when he saw Erich's high rank, and there was now a trace of doubt in his eyes. 'I still cannot release the vehicle, sir,' he said. 'The order is simple; to do so would be a court martial offence.'

'Is there a telephone inside your hut, soldier?'

The man nodded and opened the door to admit him. As he stepped into the room, Erich glanced upwards. 'Why is that light so dull?' he said. The sentry's eyes followed his gaze, and Erich hit him with a tremendous blow to the solar plexus that took him completely by surprise and drove the breath from his lungs. Before he could react, Erich grabbed his head and twisted it savagely, breaking his neck, before lowering him gently to the floor.

He quickly looked around; there was no one in sight. Suddenly, the phone buzzed. He stood petrified. Should he answer? The phone buzzed again. Erich's imagination was working overtime now. The phone buzzed again; it sounded impatient. If he answered, could he pass himself off as the sentry? Was this a routine check?

If he did not answer, how soon would it take for them to come to investigate? He answered just as it buzzed for the fourth time.

'*Ja.*'

'Willie, routine check. *Alles in ordnung?*'

'*Ja.*'

'Where were you? Why did you take so long?'

'*Ich ging für pissen.*'

There was a pause, then: '*Weitermachen.*'

Erich breathed a sigh of relief. He arranged the body so that it looked as if there was a sentry in the hut by propping him against the small desk under a window, picked up the machine pistol and switched off the light before raising the barrier and riding quietly away.

He knew of an abandoned warehouse by the river, and he went there to check out his booty. The box was locked! They attached a padlock to the hasp of the box. He considered firing his pistol into the lock, but that was something only the hero in a film would do. He looked around the abandoned building, finally locating a crowbar. It was badly bent and rusted, but it was good enough to break open the lock.

When he peered into the box, all he saw was an oilskin-wrapped parcel. He lifted it out. *Mein Gott!* It was heavy! As he unrolled the oilskin, he saw it was a statue of a gilded bird. He took a sharp breath at the size of the emerald. By the weight, it must be pure gold! Now they had their bankroll for Switzerland! Then he noticed the eyes of the bird. It was an eagle with small emeralds for eyes. It looked stunning.

As he sat on the cold concrete floor, he realised a faint smell, a musty and slightly foetid smell. It reminded him of his grandfather's pigeon loft near Spandau. A tingling started in his spine. He had the feeling that there was another presence in the old building, something evil; he could almost reach out and touch it, it had become so pervasive.

*I should get out of here*, he thought. He went to gather up the statue and froze. The thing was looking at him! The eyes had swivelled towards him and they contained such malevolence that he almost stopped breathing. *It must be the poor light and my feverish imagination*, he thought. Swiftly, he wrapped the statue and left the warehouse. He made his way to his apartment and stowed the package in a small cupboard where it was not obvious to the casual observer, and rode towards the Black Hat as far as he dared. He pushed the bike and the machine pistol into the dark river, before making his way to the club on foot.

Noni was waiting for him, looking as beautiful as ever. 'I have discovered something that will solve our problems,' he said. 'Come with me now so I can show you. Then we will discuss what we must do.'

## Gestapo Headquarters, 11 rue de Saussaies, Paris, France, 1940

*Untersturmführer* Johann Muller put down the handpiece and relaxed at his desk. When Willie did not answer his call, he had become worried. He was only young, twenty years old, and this was his first posting. Muller had dreaded this moment, when, for the first time, he was duty officer, responsible for everything in this large and important building. He hoped nothing would go wrong on his shift.

An hour later, he made his security calls to all the sentry posts again. This time Willie did not answer at all. *If he has gone to sleep*, he thought, *I'll have his balls!* He called in his duty sergeant. 'Go to the motor pool and check on the sentry. He has not answered my security check.' The sergeant went to see what that clown Willie was doing. *Don't tell me he has a woman in there with him like the last time!* Minutes later, the phone buzzed on the duty desk. Johann picked up the handpiece and, as he listened to his sergeant, all the colour drained from his face. He put down the handpiece, paused for a moment, and began a series of phone calls.

It took less than twenty minutes for the response squad to materialise, commanded by a hard-faced *Hauptsturmführer*. He relieved Johann of his duty and placed him in an interview room. He would face the commanding officer in the morning. In the meantime, there were things to do. The *Hauptsturmführer* immediately had a bulletin radioed throughout the city giving the details of the missing motorbike and then started to interview the entire duty roster.

## The Apartment of Standartenführer Erich Borden, 102 Rue Parfisal, Paris, 1940

Erich and Noni entered the apartment in a state of high excitement. He had told her in the taxi that he had found something of immense value, but nothing more than that, so that when he unwrapped the statue and placed it upon a table, she could not believe what she was seeing. '*Mon Dieu!* It is exquisite! It must be pure gold. Look at the lustre and look at the enormous emerald. It must be worth a fortune all by itself! What are we going to do?'

'There is no chance that we could sell it here in France,' he said, 'but in Switzerland, we will realise its value as a collectible. In America, it might be worth more than a million dollars.'

'*C'est vrai*, the emerald alone would be worth it.' Her eyes glowed, and she breathed a little quicker than normal. 'Come, *mon amour*, let us celebrate our good fortune, let us make love here by the statue. Soon we will be gone from this city, gone from the war.'

She unbuttoned her blouse, revealing her beautiful breasts under the thin chemise. Already her nipples were prominent against the silk. Erich wanted to have her there right now, but he suppressed his desire. 'No, we must decide what we are to do. There will be a lifetime of loving for us, but we must get out of here now. It will not be long before they are onto us.'

She looked a little sulky but had to agree. Behind her on the table, the eyes of the eagle shone with amused contempt.

## Gestapo Headquarters, 11 rue de Saussaies, Paris, France, 1940

The hard-faced *Hauptsturmführer* did not take long to find out who had been in the building two hours ago. He questioned the sentries mercilessly. The two on the front door reported several officers had entered the building. Their identity cards were in order. Besides, two were familiar to the sentries, and both had left by the front entrance about thirty minutes after they arrived. One other had not.

'It was *Standartenführer* Borden,' said one of them. 'He is that officer just arrived from Berlin on special duties. He oversees an internal investigation.'

'I know who he is. Quickly, search the building. See if he is still here!' The search revealed that the Standartenführer was indeed missing. Can it be him who stole the bike and killed the sentry? mused the Hauptsturmführer. No, it cannot be. He has a direct authority from Reichsführer Himmler himself! He is beyond reproach, and someone of my rank cannot question him. Suddenly, this had become a problem for a much higher authority.

The Hauptsturmführer made a reluctant phone call to the commander of the Paris SS, Gruppenführer Alfred von Diesnberg. Then he ordered a complete and microscopic search of the building while he waited for the senior officer to arrive.

The search revealed that nothing was missing, no files, no weapons, no sensitive documents and no money. As the reports came in, the Hauptsturmführer became increasingly confused. What would it be missing that would cause a senior officer to kill a sentry? Had the man gone mad, what did he hope to achieve? One of his men interrupted him. 'I think you should see this, sir. It looks as though we have rats in the building.' Tell me something I don't know, he thought, and the biggest rat of all just killed a sentry and stole a motorbike!

They led him to an upper level. There, on the floor, he saw the unmistakable rat droppings, just a few of them, hard up against the wall. Curious, he thought, why just a few? Were the rats constipated? He looked up and saw the trapdoor. 'What is in there?' he demanded.

The soldier stared blankly at him. 'For Christ's sake you Dummkopf, get a ladder and look!'

When he discovered the storage space recently disturbed, he knew that whatever they had concealed there the culprit had wanted. He returned to the ground floor just in time to greet his commander.

Gruppenführer Alfred von Diesnberg now had a problem on his hands. The missing Standartenführer was the prime suspect, but what was he carrying? What had he removed from that dusty storage spot?

Mein Gott! The man carried a letter from the Reichsführer himself! A terrifying reality struck him. He would have to telephone Himmler about this matter, and one did not telephone that man with unwelcome news. He had a horrible habit of shooting the messenger – literally! Gruppenführer von Diesnberg at first issued an order for the arrest of Standartenführer Borden and any others found in his company.

Finally, reluctantly, he turned to the telephone. His career may well hang on the next few minutes of conversation.

## The Apartment of Standartenführer Erich Borden, 102 Rue Parfisal, Paris, 1940

They had made for *Strasbourg*. There they could reach Switzerland through some forested area in the mountains. No one would question Erich's letter. It came from the highest authority. They packed up a few possessions and caught a taxi to the *Gare de l'Est*. As they drew away from their street, they saw a *Kubelwagen* and two black Mercedes heading back the way they had come. They had blaring horns and flashing lights.

At once, Erich knew they were in trouble. It surprised him just how quickly they had singled him out. He cursed the swift action of the response group. It meant now that his authority from Himmler was useless, and he would be a fugitive with all troops, police and the Gestapo on his trail. Erich did not want to frighten Noni with this new set of circumstances, so he told her nothing. He had to pray that they could get on a train before his letter became not a free pass, but a death warrant.

At the *Gare de l'Est*, there was no trouble with tickets. He purchased a first-class sleeping compartment for the trip to Strasbourg; then he dragged a protesting Noni into another taxi and asked the driver to take him to the *Gare de Lyon*, where they would take a train to Lausanne. They would leave the train at the last station in France and attempt the crossing, either over the lake or through the forest. They held each other as the train pulled out of the station and gathered speed. Now they had a chance.

## Gestapo Headquarters, 11 rue de Saussaies, Paris, France, 1940

*Gruppenführer* von Diesnberg lifted the receiver with a trembling hand and placed a call to the office of the *Reichsführer* in Berlin. Despite the chilly night, he was sweating, and his cap band felt several sizes too small.

By the time they made the connection, Diesnberg had decided to be forthright in his report to the *Reichsführer*. '*Heil Hitler,*' he said, 'I am afraid I have some shocking news to impart, *Herr Reichsführer*. Your emissary, *Standartenführer* Borden, has committed a crime here. He has killed a guard and stolen a motorbike. We could not find him or the bike.' He hoped that by describing Borden as Himmler's man, they could sheet home some of the blame for what had happened on the *Reichsführer* himself.

There was a momentary silence on the line. Diesnberg could hear his own heart beating. Himmler replied. 'Why would he do such a thing? He is my best man. There must be some other explanation. He was on a special mission for me, in secret. What else do you know about this incident?'

'*Herr Reichsführer*, he may carry something of value. We do not know what, but he disturbed a storage compartment. Perhaps there was something there that he wanted.'

The silence on the line seemed to exude something sinister, even evil. Diesnberg felt icy sweat trickle down his sides. Still, there was no response. '*Herr Reichsführer*, are you there?'

'Tell me about this storage compartment, *Gruppenführer*. Describe it to me in intimate detail.' The voice now was soft, full of menace, like an executioner's might be. When he heard the description, Himmler could not believe it. He could not conceive of anyone disobeying his order. *You are a dead man, Borden. You will die in great pain, and I will watch with great satisfaction*, he thought. As for the Paris office, he cursed their stupidity and determined to make an example of them.

'*Gruppenführer*, you will return to Berlin immediately. You will bring with you all who were on duty when this incident occurred. You will all report to me directly.'

Diesnberg went very pale. '*Ja, natürlich Herr Reichsführer, Heil Hitler!*' He knew it was the end of his career. He would be lucky to escape with his life. He replaced the receiver and issued his orders.

## On board the Paris-Lausanne train

They could resist no longer. The excitement of their newly discovered wealth, the adrenalin they had spent avoiding arrest and detection, had filled them with a sexual energy they had never experienced.

They tore at each other's clothing, kissing and moaning. He lifted her skirt and pulled off her underwear; he could not wait to be with her, inside her. She cried out and writhed under him, moaning and babbling words of love, until they climaxed in a way they had never done before. Afterwards, she wanted to repeat the experience; she was so aroused. After an hour, spent, their minds returned to their present difficulties.

'We must get off the train before the Swiss border,' he said. 'We must prepare now. Change into casual pants and coat, the darker the colour the better. I will try to disguise my uniform. They will look for a *Standartenführer*. I will give them something else.' He removed his uniform coat and took all the medal ribbons from it. He removed the two gold 'pips' from each shoulder strap and the runes from the collars. It now showed him as a nondescript *Sturmbannführer*. It would not pass a critical examination, but it was the best he could do. He tore up Himmler's letter and let the wind whip the pieces out the open window. After, they removed the statue from its oilskin wrapping. It gleamed in the dull light of the compartment. They both gazed in wonder at the great emerald orb and the golden wings. Then they lay in the bunk bed and tried to sleep. Their adventures and lovemaking left them exhausted, and sleep came to them almost immediately.

## French Air Space, Near Lyon, 1940

Flight Sergeant Alun Williams was lost. Not just lost, *totally* lost. He had taken off in his Whitley bomber on an operation to attack the munitions factory near Troyes. Almost from take-off, things went wrong. They had not crossed the channel when the rear gunner reported his turret would not rotate to port. Soon after, the radio operator reported that his set would not receive. The observer went aft to try to rectify the problems. They fixed the radio, but not before missing a warning about a thirty-knot tailwind.

The weather was foul with rain and sleet. They had droned on across the French countryside until they had exceeded the ETA target by thirty minutes. Williams was young and inexperienced; this was just his second operation. Finally, they flew out of the weather into bright moonlight. He called up his navigator. 'Freddie, where the hell are we?' He could see the ground now, covered in snow, so that buildings and roads stood out in sharp relief. He could see what looked like a major railway running roughly north to south.

The navigator had no answers, except to say that maybe they were too far east. Williams decided to cut his losses. He banked towards the railway line. 'Put our bombs down on that railway line, Johnny,' he said. The observer opened the bomb bay doors, issued instructions to his pilot for the bombing run and dropped the entire load. Williams completed his turn onto a reciprocal course for home, put down the nose, and pushed his throttles forward to full speed.

In the early years of the war, the RAF had a poor record for hitting its targets. In fact, many aircraft failed to find the target at all, and up to eighty per cent dropped their bombs kilometres from the aiming point. But not so tonight; Williams' bombs fell in a perfect straddle across the line. One was a direct hit, destroying both lines for over fifty yards. Williams never knew. He ran out of fuel and put down in a field short of the coast, set fire to his aircraft and set off in a fruitless attempt to reach safety. He and his crew would be guests of the *Luftwaffe* for the next four and a half years.

## On board the Paris-Lausanne train

Erich came awake with a start. For a moment, it disorientated him before he realised they were still on the train, still safe, as it charged south for the Swiss border. But something was strange; once more he could smell his grandfather's pigeon loft, a mix of ammonia, dust and feathers. It was just for a moment before the air seemed to return to normal. He looked at the statue.

'*Himmel!*' he swore. The statue had gone! No, not gone, but on the windowsill as though looking out. *Mien Gott!* Erich was sure that he had left it on the small shelf above the washstand. He had! He was sure he had!

He snatched up the eagle and wrapped it in the oilskin. Suddenly, he could have sworn the eyes turned to look at him. Once more, the glare of hatred and pure evil fell upon him. He recoiled from the sight, crying, '*Nein, nein*, it cannot be!' He seized the statue and wrapped it tightly in the oilskin. He could not look at those eyes again. Was he going mad? Or was he just imagining things? It had all felt more than real to him.

Suddenly, he felt the train slowing. There was a long and tortured scream of steel on steel as the brakes locked up, and he could hear crashing from the front of the train. The compartment tilted, throwing him to the floor, and the lights went out. He felt the car slam onto its side and drag along the ground. Everywhere came the sounds of destruction, glass shattering, people screaming, cars breaking up. The train stopped.

He could hear hissing as steam escaped the boiler, the cries of the injured, harsher voices as the officials and troops on board tried to take control of the situation. After that, the fires started.

The crash momentarily stunned Erich. He tried to rise but felt something heavy across his legs and lower torso. It was Noni, thrown from the bunk as the train slowed. *Noni! Noni! Please be unhurt*. He reached for her, but she was limp and unresponsive. He hauled her up to his chest and lifted her head to face him. It was now that he knew he was going mad. He screamed and screamed and screamed; then fainted. A few moments later he came to and saw that he was not mad. He had seen what he had seen.

The girl was dead, eyes missing, great strips of flesh torn from her face and her upper chest. He looked at the sockets where her beautiful eyes had been, her almost unrecognisable face, the damage to her beautiful breasts, and he knew he was as good as dead, too. He must get away from the dreaded statue!

Leaving the oilskin package behind, he clawed his way out of the compartment onto the ground, crazed by his desire to get away from that dreadful sight. Without looking, he ran away from the wreck as fast as he could. Behind him, he left his cap and greatcoat. He did not realise how cold it was out in the snow. He ran until he could run no longer, and he stumbled to a halt and looked back into the night.

He could see flashing lights and hear machinery working away at the site of the train wreck; he could not go back there. The fear rose in him again, pumping more adrenalin into his bloodstream.

He turned to run again, this time in a stumbling and uncontrolled manner. An hour later, he had run his race. Erich fell face down in the snow and could not rise for some time. He felt almost frozen. There were numb patches on his face and he could not feel his ears. Erich knew he was suffering from the initial stages of frostbite. He must seek some sort of help! He shuffled further into the darkness.

A patrol found him in the daylight. He had taken his last fall and had frozen to death. He was only a hundred metres from a large farmhouse.

## The wreck of the Paris-Lausanne train

It took two days to clear the wreckage of the train and repair the line. Twenty people had died in the crash and over fifty injured.

Noni's body caused the police to open an enquiry because of her wounds, and the Gestapo became involved when they finally identified her from documents in her luggage. They quickly established that she had been close to Borden, and when they identified his body, they reported the matter to Berlin as they had been told to do. Himmler had a moment of relief when he heard this news. The golden eagle must have been aboard the train with them. A search of the wreckage must surely find it! But they found no trace.

Himmler had the young *Untersturmführer* executed for 'dereliction of duty', and the entire watch individually demoted and sent to the most inhospitable posts the *Reichsführer* could find. They demoted *Gruppenführer* Diesnberg to *Standartenführer* and posted him to the freezing north of Norway. Two days later he put his pistol in his mouth and blew away the back of his head.

The first move for Himmler was the interrogation of all the rescue crews that had attended the train wreck. No one knew anything, but one man was missing and had been since the night of the crash.

Henri Blumme was a junior firefighter called to the train wreck with his crew on that fateful night. It was he who discovered the statue of the golden eagle and the mutilated body of the woman in compartment 7E. He could not believe his eyes. '*Mon Dieu!*' he said to himself, looking at the woman. 'This is surely the work of the devil!' He could smell a strange musty odour in the compartment, but he took no notice of it. When his eyes fell upon the statue, his mouth fell open with surprise. He could have sworn that there was a look of triumph in the bird's green eyes.

He tried to pick it up, and the weight told him it was solid gold; he almost became giddy when he saw the great emerald. *I am rich*, he thought, *I am rich!* He placed the eagle in his voluminous haversack and took it with him at the end of his shift. He concealed it in his basement and spent some time thinking about what to do with it. Henri was thirty years old. When France mobilised in 1939, he avoided conscription because of his job as a firefighter, considered a reserved occupation. But he was not a contented man.

He hated the Germans and yearned for their defeat. Most of his fellows felt the same way, and they were always tardy and inefficient when called out to a fire in any German establishment. But Henri's biggest problem was the shrew of a woman he had married.

They had killed her first husband in the Ardennes, right at the start of the invasion, leaving her with two little children. Henri still could not believe he had married her. He had known her from their school days. She was a pretty woman, and he had lusted after her when they were younger. Now he made her his own, and he pursued her with reckless abandon.

However, good looks are not a good indicator of a woman's

personality, and Henri found he had snared a bitter, complaining woman who refused him sex if he transgressed her rules, rules that constantly changed. When she consented to intimacy, he found her to be less than enthusiastic about it. He longed to get away from her. Now was his chance!

He knew that to come forward with his find would bring the authorities down on his head, and he knew he could not sell the statue in France. The Germans were looting anything of value. They had even stripped the Musée du Louvre of many of its outstanding works. Finally, he decided he must get to Switzerland. The border was not far away, and he could disappear into the forest and find a way across. The next night he stole his neighbour's motorcycle and set out.

The very next morning, before daybreak, the Gestapo came for him. They found two small children and a waspish woman who assailed them with invective. But she could not dismiss these men with her sharp tongue, and she could not control their behaviour with the refusal of sexual favours. They took her away for questioning. She claimed to know nothing about her husband's whereabouts or any 'special package'. After her painful interrogation, she had still not revealed anything. Himmler ordered her shot; they shot the children too.

### Lac Léman, French-Swiss border, 1940

Henri knew he had to get across the border somehow. On his long ride to the south, it surprised him that there was no pursuit; he had expected that the stolen motorcycle would be reported. He did not know that his neighbour had himself stolen the machine some months before and he was going nowhere near the police about that matter!

He considered his options on the long ride and decided that crossing the lake might be a better idea than braving the forest. He was no woodsman, but he knew a little about boats. Henri had sailed on this very body of water as a younger man. Surely, he could steal a boat!

About a mile from the lake shore, near the small town of Évian-les-Bains, he stopped and concealed the motorcycle in a large thicket of scrubby bushes and small trees. He took his haversack and checked its contents. He had placed the statue in a canvas sack. It was well past midnight, and the woods were dark and quiet.

He took the statue out of the sack for a last look before he attempted the ultimate stage of the journey. He marvelled at its beauty, especially the large emerald. What would that be worth? A king's ransom! How lucky he had stumbled upon it. He froze! *Mon Dieu!* The bird was looking at him.

He was sure that he had seen the eyes swivel in its head, looking directly at him. It was a look of pure evil that drilled into his soul. His breath caught, and he felt as though he would faint. He thrust the statue back into the sack and tied it securely. He did not know it, but he would never look upon it again.

It was a long walk into the town. Henri was nervous and inclined to jump at the slightest sound. He could still see the look in the bird's eyes. He paused and calmed himself. The task before him would not be easy. He had to have his wits about him. By now it was about two in the morning. He was not worried about that. The long winter night would give him plenty of time; it would not be light until about eight. He could cross the lake in a few hours if he could find a motorboat. There would be sentries, he knew, but he hoped they would be mostly Vichy border guards. There would be Germans too, of course; he trusted his luck that they would be few.

He carefully made his way into the outskirts of the town and moved around it towards the lake. It had grown freezing, and when he reached the lakeshore, he could see a crusting of ice that reached out about three metres from the pebble beach. He could see no boats at all along this stretch of shore. *Merde!* He would have to move along to the next inlet. Here he found several small rowboats drawn up on the beach and a small cabin cruiser moored about fifty meters from the shore. *Perfect,* he nodded to the black night. He cast around for anything that would reveal a sentry but could see none. He watched for twenty minutes, but there was no movement, no lights, no sudden glow of a cigarette. Across the lake, he could see the distant lights of neutral Switzerland, about ten miles away. He was so close. Surely nobody could stop him now.

He eased across the strand to the nearest rowboat. He would need it, for the water would be very cold, and he would sink with the weight of the statue in any case. His heart sank. There were no oars in the boat, a simple security measure against theft that he should have remembered. He moved to the next, and the next. *Merci à Dieu.* This one had oars. He slung his sack into the boat and pushed it towards the water. It was an arduous task, and by the time he got the boat to the lakeshore, he was blowing hard. He had to push it out through the icy crust, wetting himself up to the knees with freezing water. Struggling into the boat, he unshipped the oars and rowed out to the cabin cruiser. Before he boarded, he waited, searching the cruiser for any sign of a watchman. Finally, he swung his sack over the gunnel and boarded the vessel.

It was silent. He could see the town, crouching like a large black animal on the shore, but there were no lights showing, no sign of pursuit. Henri carried his sack into the cabin and peered around in the darkness for the boat's control panel. He moved to the bow and let the mooring rope go, pushing the boat away from its buoy with a long boat hook. It cleared the buoy and floated a little towards the open lake before he started the engine. It made a dreadful racket, but he could do nothing about that.

He swung the bows towards Switzerland and moved slowly at an idle away from the shore. Still, there were no lights showing in the town. About two hundred metres from the shore, he pushed the throttle forward to maximum speed. He guessed the boat should make eight knots at least, but it seemed responsive and faster than that. For the first time since he had discovered the statue, he relaxed.

Just as he did so, he heard a harsh voice from behind him, '*Was machst du? Stoppen sie das boot!*' He turned to see a German soldier pointing a rifle at him. So, there *was* a watchman. He must have been asleep and awoke to the sound of the engine as he had sped up. Henri reached out and cut the throttle. He stared at the German as the way fell off the boat and it came to a halt, rocking slightly in the breeze.

Henri spoke little German, so he waited for the other man to speak. 'You are trying to escape, *nein?* Are you a Jew or just a criminal?' Henri remained silent. The man moved towards him. 'Move away from the controls. We are returning to shore. The Gestapo will be interested in you. *Schnell!*'

Henri could see his dream was about to evaporate, his statue confiscated, himself in a cell, tortured and awaiting execution. He was desperate. He knew he would not go back, could not go back; he must regain control of the boat. What could he do? He would have to overpower this man, take a chance on the rifle, and try to grab it before he could fire. Then the soldier made a fatal mistake. A rifle is not a suitable weapon in a confined space, especially a long one; it is unwieldy and gets caught on any obstruction. At close quarters, it can be an encumbrance. But the German compounded the error by moving closer. Henri dived at him.

The soldier squeezed his trigger in a reflex action. Henri felt the wind of the bullet's passage as it almost creased his shoulder; it ricocheted off the cabin's steel wall and buried itself in his side, but he hardly felt the strike; he was fighting for his life, in the dark, on the floor of the cabin.

The German was strong, and he repeatedly punched Henri in the face and neck, but his helmet came loose and fell across his eyes. Henri took the advantage and subdued him with a flurry of blows.

He staggered to his feet. Across the water he could see some lights coming on and a siren began to wail. *Merde!* They will be coming for him! He stumbled to the controls and opened the throttle as far as he could.

Pretty soon he saw flares rise above the lake. *They will have some kind of patrol boat,* he thought, *armed, and a damned sight faster than this boat is.* He could do nothing more than steer for the far shore. Fifteen minutes later, he saw a searchlight beam sweeping the surface of the lake. They were too far away to see him yet, but he knew they were closing fast.

He felt dizzy and for the first time noticed the pain in his side. He felt up and down his body. Blood soaked his clothes; it was still seeping down his side. He must have lost a lot, he realised. He took his handkerchief and stuffed it up under his shirt to staunch the flow.

Behind him, the searchlight was creeping closer. Ten minutes later, its beam washed over the stern of his boat. Another couple of minutes and he saw glowing balls of tracer coming towards him from the boat's deck-mounted cannon. He put his helm hard over, and the tracer flashed past. Immediately he turned the other way, once more avoiding the fire. However, this was an unequal battle and eventually, he felt the thump of strikes on his stern, and the rattle of fragments hitting the wheelhouse. Another burst crashed into the stern. He felt the motor hesitate, slow down and pick up again. A cannon shell smashed into the wheelhouse. He felt a terrible blow on his right shoulder, flinging him into the windshield. It could not be long before they caught him. He collapsed against the wheel, his hand still holding the throttle at full speed, waiting for the end.

Suddenly, the firing stopped, and the searchlight shut down. He was not to know that he had crossed the line from French to Swiss territory in the middle of the lake. He had time to register the quiet before he collapsed, unconscious, to the floor. The boat continued, forging on across the water towards Switzerland.

Eventually, the motor stuttered to a halt. The boat drifted slowly down the lake to the east and, just before daybreak, it nosed into a small mud beach near the town of Nyon, in Switzerland, and came to a halt. Henri lay on the cabin floor. He had bled to death. At the last moment, he reached out to the sack in a futile attempt to look once more at the treasure he would never spend. Beside him was the German soldier. He was dead too, killed by the cannon fire.

## Near Nyon, Switzerland, 1940

Marcus Nilande lived with his family on a small farm on the lakeside near Nyon. He had developed a habit of rising early and exploring the waterline. Over the years, he had discovered many things he could make use of. This morning, however, he made the find of his life.

He approached the boat without caution, just youthful curiosity. As he neared the vessel, he could see that the wheelhouse and transom bore damage from heavy gunfire. When he climbed into the wheelhouse, he took one look and stumbled to the railing to vomit. He ran all the way home and told his father, who went down to the lake himself, to see what he might salvage before he informed the police about the incident. He found little of value, just some tins of food and some dry goods in the saloon. But he saw the canvas sack and tried to pull it out from under one of the bodies. It was very heavy, and he struggled to retrieve it, but when he dragged it out to the open deck into better light to examine it properly, it stupefied him to discover the statue. The shining gold and the enormous emerald were things he had never imagined. The little wheels in his head calculated the value, but the figures were too much for this peasant farmer to believe. He put the statue back in the sack and took it home.

There was a small cavity under the floor of his ancient cow shed. He did not know its purpose – made perhaps a hundred years ago – but now it served as the perfect place to conceal something of immense value. He shovelled cow dung and bedding straw across the trapdoor until there was no sign of it. He cycled into the town to telephone the police about the boat.

## SS Headquarters, Prinz Albrechtstrasse 108, Berlin, 1941

*Der Reichsführer-SS* put down his telephone, filled with a rage so great it threatened to blow the top off his head. He had been speaking to the SS in Lyon, and the news had been all bad. By now they were certain that this *verdammte* fireman had the 'special package', but just where he had taken it was a mystery.

Himmler had ordered a thorough investigation of the man, including a search of his premises, the interrogation of his family, and all the neighbours and friends of the man. His men had dealt with the family and were well through the interrogation process without result. The *Hauptsturmführer* in charge spent some time in deep thought before issuing an order to bring in the neighbour Giles Montue for further questioning; he had been less than convincing with his previous answers, and the *Hauptsturmführer* remembered he had looked shifty and uncomfortable.

It terrified Giles when the SS came for him again. He was a railway porter and a petty criminal. He had been pilfering from passengers' luggage for many years. As well, there was the business of the stolen motorcycle. Following 'questioning' with the assistance of two large SS troopers armed with batons and equally large fists, all his resistance collapsed, and he told them of the motorcycle that had disappeared on the night his neighbour had also disappeared. His reluctance to answer had cost the SS a day. The fugitive must be a long way away by now. Giles did not have to worry about his motorcycle for long; after lunch, they shot him.

Soon reports came in from Évian-les-Bains of the stolen boat, the missing sentry, and the futile chase across the lake. An hour later, they found the missing motorcycle. *So,* thought Himmler, *the schwien had made it to Switzerland! It would be difficult, if not impossible, to retrieve it from there.* He picked up the telephone and gave instructions that the commander at Évian-les-Bains and the captain of the patrol boat report to Berlin immediately. He would deal with them himself.

He made a second call to the office of the Gestapo and arranged a meeting with the officer responsible for liaison with the Abwehr, the secret intelligence section. He put him on notice that an international operation might be necessary.

By this time, *Der Reichsführer-SS* had become obsessed with the golden eagle. Common sense should have told him he should cut his losses, but he was a stubborn man. Unfortunately for him, his men were aware of Himmler's propensity to execute anyone he thought had failed him. That evening, the commander and the entire patrol boat crew embarked and headed for Switzerland, where they sought political asylum.

## Lausanne, Switzerland, 1941

Hans Langer and Peter Schwartz sat outside a café on the shores of Lac Leman, drinking real coffee and enjoying the pleasant spring day. The view of the lake was remarkable. Here in Switzerland, people went about their business without fear. There were many sailboats on the lake, skimming across the sparkling water, and a flotilla of white swans glided by, eyes on the jetties for tourists with bread to throw to them. What a contrast it was to Berlin! Both men did not know about the impending Operation *Barbarossa*, although they were aware there was something big in the offing. They were excluded from that, because Admiral Canaris had selected them himself to carry out this mission. The Abwehr had warned them that *Reichsführer* Himmler had an abiding interest and had sworn them to secrecy.

They were to seek a 'special package' containing a valuable golden eagle, the property of the Reich that had been misappropriated by a French fireman who had stolen it and a boat and tried to get across the lake to Switzerland. The man and the boat had been found, but the package was missing. A patrol boat had transported the men to the Swiss side of the lake in the dead of night, engines muffled, flying a Swiss flag. They possessed passports and documentation that showed them to be Swiss businessmen from Zurich. They were to pose as friends on holiday together. *How appropriate*, thought Hans, *that is just what we will be!* They had codes and the names of a contact at the German Embassy to whom they would report weekly. Right now, they were polishing up their cover by posing as tourists. They were in no hurry to find out anything. The RAF had bombed Berlin, pathetic attempts really, but you never knew if a stray bomb was going to spoil your day.

Besides, the weather there was still cold and miserable, and there were shortages of some foods. They were glad to be here. Before the war, both had been detectives in the city police, drafted into their present roles. Neither were Nazis nor were they enthusiastic about the war. But they *were* hard men, forged in the crucible of the chaos that preceded the election of Hitler. Corruption, death and brutality were no strangers to them.

They were discussing where they would eat lunch. It was a tough decision. Afterwards, they might take a lake cruise. And tonight … well, there were plenty of bars and pretty girls.

## SS Headquarters, Prinz Albrechtstrasse 108, Berlin, 1941

It infuriated Himmler. There had been no noteworthy progress from Switzerland, and months had elapsed since the men had landed. They reported they had been to *Geneva* and *Zurich* without luck. At present, they were trying to form a relationship with a police inspector, hoping they could get more information about the boat the Frenchman had stolen.

The information they had been seeking had been available from the time they had reported the boat to Swiss police. It was a delicate matter and the stolid Swiss were not about to rush into anything. One problem was that the boat was the property of the Vichy government. At first, the Swiss would deal only with them. The Vichy, on the other hand, knew nothing about the golden eagle. They assumed it was a minor matter of two men seeking refuge from the war. There was no reason at all to inform the SS about it.

The invasion of Russia had begun, and Himmler found himself terribly busy. His *Einsatzgruppen* and *SS* battalions were gathering up all the Jews they could find in the conquered territories, and there were many. They had to shoot and bury them all, and the task was proving too much for his men. There were instances of psychosis and reluctance to take part from some of them. Those usually ended up in the pits with the Jews. Moreover, it was using a lot of ammunition and a tug of war for supplies was developing with the army.

At first, the invasion was successful. The element of surprise caught out the Russian army, disorganised by Stalin's purges of officers before the war, poorly equipped and badly led, and it fell back in disarray, leaving the Germans with countless prisoners.

Eventually, the Russians would halt and repulse the Germans, but that was more than a year away and not until they were only forty kilometres from Moscow.

In the meantime, the invasion diverted Himmler's attention from the golden eagle, and the French still did not know that their boat was of any importance to the SS. Late in the summer, someone from the SS thought to ask the French about it.

## Geneva, Switzerland, 1941

Langer and Schwartz had made a break. The Swiss police inspector they had been cultivating had finally delivered. He had agreed to provide them with a copy of the file about the boat incident. It was going to cost them a goodly sum, but Berlin had agreed. The Inspector had already suspected that he was dealing with Germans but did not give any indication of that. He had picked them for interlopers within minutes, for he had heard Prussian accents before. His own country's security did not concern him. *Mein Gott*, he thought, *if the rest of their spies are as good as these, we have nothing to worry about*. However, it would be a great chance to give his complaining wife the new sofa she had wanted for months.

When the Germans had read the file, they set off for Nyon as soon as possible. They booked into an inn and asked questions. Posing as newspapermen and offering to publish anyone who remembered the story, they soon found out where the boat had grounded and visited the nearby farms and houses. The file from the Swiss police said that an anonymous telephone call had notified them. That was all they could tell them.

'It has to be someone near the shore,' said Hans. 'They would be the first persons to see the boat that morning.'

They canvassed the houses for a mile in each direction, without luck, and adjourned for lunch. As they ate, they discussed the morning's work. 'Someone must have seen it early on,' said Peter. 'I am inclined to return to that farmer, Nilande. He looked a bit furtive to me, maybe he is hiding something.'

## The Nilande Farm, near Nyon, Switzerland, 1941

Roger Nilande was at home with his eighteen-year-old daughter, Helga, who had been his housekeeper since his wife had died a year ago; Marcus was at the village school.

He looked out from the kitchen window, surprised to see the two newspaper men approaching. *What do they want now? I told them everything I am going to this morning.* He greeted them brusquely. Hans did the talking. '*Herr* Nilande,' he said, 'I fear that you have not been frank with us. You are the nearest to the lake here. You must have seen the boat that morning.'

'So, I did,' he said, 'but that was much later. I was milking the cows and only heard about it when the police arrived.'

'That is a lie. We know you must have seen it first thing. It was sitting right there. You would have seen it from your front window as soon as you woke.'

'No, no, I was at the cowshed. It is behind the house. I could not have seen it.'

'Enough,' said Hans, drawing a pistol. 'We will have the truth now or the consequences will be dire for you!'

Roger worried now. His eyes darted from one to the other and back to Helga. 'Who are you? What do you want?'

'We believe you have a valuable object that you removed from the boat before the police arrived. It is the property of the Reich, stolen by the man in the boat. We must have it now. Quickly, where is it? Bring it to us now or you will give up your life. You are nothing compared to the importance of that object. We will have no alternative but to shoot you if you do not tell us.'

Roger, frightened now, reasoned that they would not kill him before they had the package. 'I do not know of any object. I am a poor farmer. Do you imagine I would not sell such a thing if I were to find it?'

Hans nodded to Peter, who moved to the girl and, grabbing her blouse, tore it open to expose her breasts. A savage backhand to her face cut her scream short. 'Your daughter is a sweet fruit ripe for the picking, *mein Herr*, we could have some fun with her. Tell us now or she will get the best *fickerei* she will ever get!'

'*Nien, nien*, do not hurt her. She is only a child. I will show you the hiding place. Do not hurt her, *bitte nicht!*'

Roger took them all to the cowshed and uncovered the trapdoor, reached in, and pulled out the sack. He handed it to Peter. 'Right,' he said, 'back to the house.' In the kitchen, they tied Roger to a chair, and they dragged Helga into a bedroom. They tore off her clothes and raped her brutally several times. She did not cry out, for she did not want to distress her father. When they had finished with her, Peter put a pillow over her face and smothered her.

They returned to the kitchen. Roger looked at them with anxious, pleading eyes. 'Don't worry about your daughter, *mein freund,*' Hans said, 'she has just had the time of her life!' He shot him twice in the head.

## Dijon, France, 1941

Peter and Hans left the farm in a hurry and drove to Lausanne as quickly as they could. They purchased tickets for Paris on the next available train and left within the hour. At the frontier, they presented the German Diplomatic passports the Abwehr had provided and passed through immediately. They settled down for the run to Paris, tired and sleepy, for they had a long day and spent a lot of energy.

They had not looked in the sack, but they could tell by its weight that there must be a large golden object inside. When dusk fell, they drew the curtains and carefully lifted the statue from its container. Both almost stopped breathing. They could not believe what they were seeing. 'See that emerald,' said Peter. 'I have never even dreamed of something like that, and there must be a fortune in the gold alone. I wonder what it is,' Hans said he had seen pictures of similar things in books about South America, but nothing to match this. *God knows what it may be worth*, he said to himself. *No wonder the Abwehr wanted it so badly.*

'Look at the eyes,' he said, 'they seem almost alive.'

Hans looked. 'He is not looking thrilled,' he said, 'almost evil, in fact.' Suddenly he started, thinking he saw the eyes move, but no, he was imagining things. He put the statue back in the sack and they both went to sleep. The train rattled on. In a few hours it would be in Dijon, before the last stage to Paris. Both men slumbered on, oblivious to what was happening around them.

Several hours later, the sound of the train's whistle woke Hans. They were close to Dijon now. The train would stop there to take on coal and water. He was looking forward to coffee. He glanced down to the sack.

*Scheiss!* The sack was empty! He knew it had contained the statue before they had slept. Then he saw it on the windowsill, as though looking out. He laughed to himself. 'Peter, *du Schwein*, you almost had me fooled,' he said, jumping down from the bunk and shaking his companion. Peter did not move. Hans bent over him to shake him again. What he saw caused him to turn to the washstand and vomit, repeatedly. Most of Peter's face was torn to bits, his eyes were missing, and he was very dead!

Terror overtook him. What has happened? He looked around. The compartment door was still locked. No one could have entered. His gaze fell upon the statue. If anyone had done this, surely, they would have stolen the eagle as well. He felt his heartbeat skyrocket; he experienced an overwhelming desire to be away from here, anywhere but here.

But they made Hans of sterner stuff. He gradually regained his composure and considered what he could do now. If he reported this, they would think that he had killed his companion. There was no other suspect. And he had the motive of the golden eagle – he had planned to steal it, they would say.

Finally, he reached a decision. He would leave the train at Dijon. If he were careful, no one would notice him. He knew he faced grim justice if he were to be arrested. Hans waited until the train stopped. He covered Peter with a blanket, picked up the eagle, and left the train, locking the compartment behind him. He did not notice the malicious look in the bird's eyes as he stuffed it into the sack and he did not notice the strange foetid, musty smell in the compartment. Neither did he see the feathers on the floor.

### Paris, France, 1941

The crew from the Lausanne train had worked a double shift; so many men taken by the Germans for forced labour, so many had not yet returned from the prisoner of war camps, that there were labour shortages everywhere. Someone shunted aside the rail cars into a service area and the train crew went home to their families. It would be two days before workers cleaned the cars and put them back into service.

When they found the body of Peter Schwartz, it took some time to identify him. It did not help the process that the passports and identity papers he carried were false.

The Vichy authorities again failed to liaise with the SS and Gestapo, and it was almost a month before they made a positive identification.

A further week elapsed before his connection to the Abwehr became apparent. It forced the Abwehr to report to the *Reichsführer-SS* that their other man and the 'special package' had disappeared somewhere around Dijon some six weeks ago.

## SS Headquarters, Prinz Albrechtstrasse 108, Berlin, 1941

Himmler's rage was legendary. This time it exceeded all previous records. He knew he should abandon the search for the statue; it was not worth the cost anymore. The Russian winter was locking the German armies in its icy grip. Hitler had expected to win easily, and they did not issue the armies with winter clothing. Their advance faltered, and they hunkered down in freezing conditions to wait for the spring. Many froze to death. But the *Reichsführer* had lost all reason with the golden eagle. He dreamed of it; it filled every idle minute he had. He must retrieve it. It had become an obsession. He called in one of his most fervent Nazi officers.

*Obersturmbannführer* Rolo Giessner was a rabid anti-Semite who had wedded himself to the Nazi cause by the time he was a seventeen-year-old member of the SA. He had fought the communists on the streets and had taken a leading role in the events of Kristallnacht, putting the torch to many Jewish shops and synagogues. In the initial stages of *Barbarossa*, he commanded an *Einsatzgruppe* and boasted that his team had eliminated almost forty thousand of *der Juden ratten*. He would die waving the Nazi flag. For him, a summons from Himmler was like a papal audience to a Catholic. He listened as Himmler told him the full story of the golden eagle, *der Steinadler*. 'I am now giving you a sacred task. You must find this object for the greater glory of *der Führer und der Reich*. You will assemble a team to complete this task, no matter how long it takes. Here is a letter signed by me giving you authority over all other Wehrmacht and SS personnel in the pursuit of your task. Go now. I will expect regular reports. You must not fail. *Heil Hitler!*'

Giessner selected twenty men and departed for France, but they had no success. Meanwhile, the fortunes of the Reich had taken a significant nosedive. In Russia, the Germans had made ground as the Russians fell back. Stalingrad was invested and the Ploesti oilfields in Romania were within reach, but the advance halted. It would go no further. In Europe, the RAF and the newly arrived US Eighth Air Force were forging an alliance that would see the beginning of the massive air raids that would eventually destroy most of Germany's great cities. In North Africa, Rommel's armies halted and in Italy, the people were sick of the war and wanted out. It would be a year or more before that happened, but things were not good. Himmler had become distracted by the enormous task of constructing the vast number of concentration camps, the ovens and the extermination of the Jews that would take place there. He rarely thought now of the golden eagle.

## The Jura, France, 1941

When Hans Langer left the train at Dijon, his first response had been to put as much distance between himself and the railway station as he could. He was not to know that he had a couple of days of grace because of the railway staff problems in Paris. He slung the heavy sack over his shoulder and walked towards the outskirts of the town.

Outside a bar, he stole a bicycle from a rack and set off to the east, towards the Swiss border. Hans kept to the back roads as much as he could. He realised that he now had no way back. They would blame him for the death of Peter Schwartz and the theft of the golden eagle.

In Germany, his life would be brief and painful. He had no options. He had some German and French currency notes, but not much of either. Hans knew he could not sell such an item as the statue. He would have to wait until after the war to do that, and that could be years. How was he to survive?

Occasionally, he called into small villages to buy food. There was not much to buy; there were shortages of almost everything except wine, bread and the local cheeses. For the first time, he appreciated the skills he had learned in the *Hitler-Jugend*, many outdoor skills of survival and living off the land. He was an excellent skier and accomplished mountaineer; he was sure he could survive in the mountains for as long as he needed to.

Two weeks later, he reached the village of Morteaux, close to the mountains of the Jura. Here he dumped the bike and bought a rough haversack, filling it with as much food as he could carry, including candles and matches. He stole a heavy coat from a rack in a bar. They would not notice it, for the weather was mild still; the owner would not be looking for it for a month or more. He set off for the mountains. He needed shelter and a water source. Two days later he found what he wanted, a survival hut, one of many built in the mountains and stocked with food and warm clothing for the assistance of lost skiers. It was near a small stream. Here he would wait out the war.

## *SS Headquarters, Prinz Albrechtstrasse 108, Berlin, 1943*

*Obersturmbannführer* Rolo Giessner had exhausted all his resources. He had to admit that the trail of the golden eagle had gone stone cold. He reported to Himmler, who recalled him to Berlin.

*Der Reichsführer* was not pleased, but he had other, more important things on his mind. In North Africa, Montgomery's victory at *el Alamein*, and the subsequent Axis retreat had resulted in the capture of a quarter of a million prisoners and the end of the *Afrika Korps. Generalfeldmarschall* Paulus had surrendered his sixth army at Stalingrad, leaving three hundred thousand dead or prisoners. Of the more than ninety thousand prisoners, only a handful would ever see Germany again. The Allies had landed in Sicily and were preparing to invade the Italian mainland. Italy was teetering and would soon sue for peace. The bombing offensive was laying waste to city after city as the RAF flew by night and the Eighth Air Force by day. Only the fanatics still believed Germany could win the war.

So, the golden eagle had moved almost to the bottom of the *Reichsführer's* list of priorities. They gave Geissner a command on the Russian front and he left Berlin on the next available train. There he found that his regiment was at half strength, half frozen and without hope. The world had indeed turned sour for *Obersturmbannführer* Rolo Giessner.

## The Jura, France, 1943

Hans Langer had survived two winters alone in the mountains. He had seen some aircraft searching but his hut remained undisturbed, for there was little recreational skiing; the war had seen to that.

He had not heard news of the war since he had arrived at the hut. He had neither cut his hair nor shaved. Hans sometimes felt that he was going mad. He had nothing to sustain his spirit. He was not a religious man, and, in any case, the crimes he had committed in the name of the Reich would bar him from any conventional version of heaven. Only the golden eagle remained. If he could survive another winter, he could surely live in luxury.

He had buried the statue under a large boulder, near to his hideout. Now he wished he had kept it in the hut, for the mere sight of it may have helped to raise his spirits, but that was too much of a risk. Hans had harvested berries in the summer, and from time to time he would descend from his hut at night and steal as much as he could carry from field and orchard. He only took a few items from each farm so that his activities remained unnoticed. He had a large mound of apples and potatoes he hoped would last out the winter.

## The Eastern Front, 1944

*Obersturmbannführer* Rolo Giessner had been given a battered battalion of mixed troops. They had been press-ganged, mostly. There were Poles and Finns and Latvians, and even some Dutch and Belgians. They were remnants of the 'foreign' divisions that were formed from Nazi admirers in the heady days of victory in 1940-41. They stiffened the regiment by approximately fifty per cent German components.

The troops were half starved and frozen. They had been retreating from the Red Army for months now and were full of fear of the Russians. They had seen what they did to prisoners. The invasion had involved many of these SS troops in rape, arson and murder in the towns they had occupied in 1941. They could expect no mercy now. They continued to fight, retreat and stand and fight again, but retreating, slowly, irrevocably, to the west, to the German border, to Berlin.

## The Jura, France, 1944

In the mountains, it was a hard winter. Hans was in much poorer shape than he had been in the previous one. He was almost skeletal now and finding it hard to maintain his body heat. He still had some food left, but not much. Hans had no way of knowing what day or date it was, despite a tally of days he had marked off against the wall. His mental state was in serious decline. He began to have dreams. Dreams not of long-ago pleasantries with his family and friends, but dreams of Jews, haggard and bleeding, being placed in trucks, of broken glass and the smell of smoke, of the dead faces, the broken bodies, and the cries of the tortured from the cells of the police stations. Increasingly often he saw the blood spurt from the head of the Swiss farmer and the silent, desperate pleas for mercy in the eyes of the girl, Helga.

Sometime in late February, he could feel the temperature begin to rise. He stumbled from his hut and retrieved the long-buried statue of the golden eagle. It was just for a look, he told himself.

Back in the hut, he polished the eagle with an old handkerchief.

It glowed warmly in the feeble light of his oil lamp, turned down to conserve the little fuel he had left. He noticed again that the thing was looking at him. He was not frightened now, as, half mad, he talked to it, long conversations of his youth in Prussia, of his days in the *Hitler-Jugend*, of his trips to the mountains to hike and climb, even of his many girlfriends and how successful he had been with them.

Finally, as the weather warmed little by little, he replaced the statue in its hiding place. He had seen the look in its eyes change and had responded to each mood he saw there. He applauded the cheerful looks, scolded the angry ones. By now, he had completely lost his mind.

Early in the spring, a small group of the French resistance, the Marquisards, stumbled across the hut. They found an emaciated man, with long hair and beard, with staring eyes, barely alive. He was rambling, muttering, speaking about Helga and Peter and a golden eagle. They took him for a deserter and his ramblings as referring to his family and the birds of prey he may have seen in the mountains. They carried him back to their main camp some miles away and fed him warm soup. Later that evening, he woke and mumbled again. His body convulsed once, and he cried out, *'Der Steinadler ist es mir! Ist es mir!'* Then he died.

They buried him there. Only a few understood enough German to know what he had said, and by that stage of the war, no one cared a fig for a German. One took his pistol as a souvenir.

## West of the Oder Fluß, on the Seelow Heights, Germany, 1945

*Obersturmbannführer* Rolo Giessner was down to a company now. There had been many casualties and more than a few desertions. Behind the lines, units of SS Feldgendarmerie arrested any soldier who did not carry written instructions permitting him to be there. These were summarily executed, mostly by hanging from the nearest tree or lamp post, bearing a placard around their necks announcing them to be traitors and enemies of the Reich.

Giessner knew that the war was lost. They all knew. They stayed only to prevent the Russians from entering Berlin, and the terrible orgy of rape and pillage that would follow. A few clung to the ridiculous belief that Hitler would make a separate peace with the British and the Americans, whereupon they would join Germany in repulsing the Russians. Others planned to move south and west and surrender to the Americans. They knew they could expect no mercy from the Russians.

Giessner gathered around him a small group of his most trusted men, all ardent Nazis like himself. They acted under the self-delusion that they could found a guerrilla movement in the alps of Bavaria, to carry on the fighting until the long-awaited secret weapons would materialise to wipe the Allies from the face of the earth. As night fell, they loaded themselves into two half-tracks whose fuel tanks they had filled with jerry cans stolen from the fuel dump and slipped away into the darkness. They headed to the south-west. They had not gone far when a *Feldgendarmerie* patrol challenged them, but Giessner's high rank and the orders he had forged got them through.

For two nights and the days that followed, they enjoyed an uninterrupted journey, but as dusk fell on the second day, four *IL-28 Sturmovik* rocket-armed ground attack aircraft fell from the sky. The first rocket destroyed the leading vehicle and a near miss blew a track off the other. In a matter of seconds, they had lost their transport.

As they scattered and dived for cover, the aircraft turned for a second pass, guns blazing, before soaring into the sky and heading east, back to their base, hot food and vodka. Only four men survived, Giessner and three others. They salvaged what food and ammunition they could and headed away to the tree line and the safety of the forest.

Two days later, they came across another *Feldgendarmerie* patrol. There was no option but to brazen it out. Giessner immediately tried to intimidate their commander, a young *Untersturmführer*, but the boy stood his ground.

'The Americans are not far down the valley,' he said, pointing to the stream below them. 'You are not by any chance planning to join them, are you?'

'You are impertinent, young man. We are an advance party to set up a defensive line here against them. Allow us to pass.'

'An advance party, just four of you? And where are your vehicles, where are your machine guns, where is your pioneer platoon? *Herr Obersturmbannführer*, please surrender your arms. I arrest you in the name of *Der Führer, Heil Hitler!*'

Giessner opened fire on the patrol. He saw the young officer fall and his own three men go down as the others opened fire. It was a short, brutal exchange. When the firing ceased, only Giessner remained standing. Two other men were alive, one of them a companion. 'I am afraid you will have to carry me, *Kamerad*,' he said, 'my leg is broken.' Giessner shot them both.

He had received a bullet in the side. It had grazed the flesh and broken a rib; it was painful but would not be too much of an inconvenience. Besides, it would make him look more authentic. His dreams of a resistance movement in Bavaria and the secret weapons were now impossible. He resolved to escape.

He followed the valley down towards the stream below. On the way, he saw plentiful evidence of the *Feldgendarmerie* in action. More than a dozen bodies were swinging from trees. He looked at each one. Finally, he found what he had been looking for, a man about his size and with roughly similar coloured hair and facial features. He cut him down and removed his clothing.

Twenty minutes later he stood as *Gefrieter* Heinrich Arner of the German army, complete with papers, wallet, identity discs, and pay book. In the wallet was a picture of a handsome young woman. *It was a pity*, he thought, *that he was not going home to her!*

There was only one thing left to do. He gathered some kindling and built a small fire. While he waited for the wood to burn down and coals to form, he took off his tunic and shirt. Like all SS members, he carried a small tattoo showing his blood group near his left armpit. One look and they would know he was SS.

The coals were forming now. He took the dead man's bayonet and heated it until it glowed red, then he dragged it across the tattoo until it obliterated the mark. The flesh shrivelled and smoked, smelling like roasting meat; the pain was almost more than he could bear, and he knew he would have to do even more. He stabbed himself in the upper arm, ribs, and armpit to disguise the remnants of the tattoo. Finally, he stood and walked down to the stream and the Americans.

# MIKE BRODIE

*Brodie's Crossing, NSW, Australia, 1995*

Brendan Brodie left Ireland in 1847. He and his four brothers set off for the new world. In Ireland, the potato famine was at its height and many were starving. On the poverty-stricken farm in County Donegal, his family could not hope to survive if they all stayed. They made their way to Cobh in County Cork, where vessels for New York sailed. That night they celebrated their decision with plentiful ale. Brendan, ever the ladies' man, disappeared with one of the bar girls. He was not in his room at daylight when the others rose and made their way to the docks.

Brendan arrived just as his ship was disappearing over the horizon. Undeterred, he booked passage on another ship. In his hungover state, he did not realise that it was bound for the colony of New South Wales, in the land that would become Australia.

Brendan's mistake was a fortuitous one. In Gulgong he found himself digging for gold and, by a stroke of luck, he unearthed a large nugget worth more than a thousand pounds. Unlike others, he did not put it all back across the bar at Fancy Mary's but quit while he was in front and headed for the great sheep runs of the north-west plains. He went to work for a squatter who drank himself to death and he gained the property by marrying the grieving widow. She was, no doubt, influenced by the intimate services he had rendered to her, which her drunken husband could not provide.

He prospered and so did subsequent generations. They purchased more land, and by 1995 Mike Brodie's family presided over more than ten thousand acres of the most fertile land in New South Wales. 'Donegal', Brendan Brodie had called it and it produced, not wool anymore, but wheat, sorghum, chickpeas, cotton, and beef.

Mike had three older brothers, so he was the runt of the litter, so to speak, and not likely to get a big share of the family property. This did not dishearten him, for he was not very keen on becoming a farmer. Instead, he wanted to study the science of Agriculture and enter the service side of the business. His father sent him down to Sydney to take his degree. In his first year, he fell deeply in love with Anna, the daughter of an immigrant Greek family. For ten months he swam in her liquid eyes and enjoyed her beautiful body. Besotted by her, he asked her to marry him and come back with him to Brodie's Crossing.

But she refused. Her father, she said, would not allow her to marry an 'un'a'civilised Auftsryan boy'. He already had selected a good Greek boy to be her husband. She did not want to marry him, but she must do what her father wanted. She would not disobey him.

She continued her torrid affair with Mike until a week before her wedding, tearfully kissed him goodbye and drove away. He never saw her again.

It devastated him. He had really loved her that much. In his second year he played the field, taking what was on offer and ignoring any romantic attachments. Burnt once; he was not anxious to repeat the experience. He gained a reputation amongst the young women of the campus as unreliable but nice, good in bed, but not husband material.

Then he met Ricki. She was tall and slim with long blonde hair, and he wanted her from the moment he saw her. Two weeks after he graduated, he married her in a small private ceremony. Looking back, he knew it was a big mistake. The girl he imagined he knew and loved became a quite different proposition as a wife. She complained constantly. She would not visit his family 'way out there in the sticks' and she shamelessly used her sexual favours to control his behaviour. Ricki had picked her mark well, for Mike had a high libido and could not outlast her. Ricki had never liked sex very much, so she did not miss it.

They were married for almost a year when the army called him up to complete his national service training. For him, the army was both a refuge and a challenge. He applied for officer training and a scant six months later, he found himself a brand new, bright and shiny Second Lieutenant, commanding a platoon of infantry in Vietnam. He was lucky. Mike had a good, regular army platoon sergeant who took him under his wing and made an outstanding officer out of him in ways so subtle Mike was scarcely aware of it.

In 1970, he returned to Australia, a captain, wearing the Military Cross, awarded for a particularly good piece of work when the Viet Cong ambushed his company. They offered him a permanent commission in the regular army, but he had seen enough of killing and army bullshit. He declined and went back to his apartment in Sydney.

The first sign of trouble was when he tried to phone Ricki from the airport. All he got was a 'number disconnected' signal. When he opened his front door, he almost fell over a pile of mail, mostly long overdue bills, but also a notice of eviction for unpaid rent. She had taken all her things and all their things. His clothes and his books were still there, but nothing else was. No car, no furniture and he quickly discovered their bank account cleaned out and closed. He only saw Ricki once more, about ten years later, as a talking head on a TV show. She was the leader of some kind of 'women's collective', her lovely hair gone, cropped close to her skull. She wore no makeup or jewellery and she was grim faced and intense, as she blamed anyone but herself for most of the world's troubles. Mike had a suspicion she may have had a lesbian lover waiting for her at home.

He left the flat and spent some of his hard-earned dollars on a train ticket to Brodie's Crossing. He spent the rest of the year on those happy acres helping his brothers and his father with the work of the farm. After Christmas he declared himself healed and applied for a job with the Department of Agriculture. They sent him to Albury where he worked as an agronomist for five years, until one day there was a phone call from Phil, his oldest brother. It changed his life.

'Come home for a week,' his brother had said. 'I think we can make a shitload of money here. I'll fill you in when you get here.' Mike packed a bag and headed north. Two days later he was sitting in Phil's lounge room drinking a cold beer. The other boys were coming for dinner.

At 'Donegal', Phil had taken over as the manager. He handled the overall management, the fiscal management and the cattle herd. Jack handled the broad acre cropping, and Robert the irrigated crops, mainly cotton.

There was a revolution happening in Australian agriculture. The age of zero-till farming was about to take off. Simply, this was the replacement of mechanical cultivation with chemical control of weeds. One of the consequences of this practice was that farmers could no longer plant the same crop in the same field year after year. They had to grow a range of crops to avoid diseases. Consequently, the management of cropping plans became increasingly complex. New and better herbicides were arriving two or three times a year. The farmers now needed someone who could keep up with the latest crop spraying and chemical technology. In short, they needed an expert agronomist like Mike.

After a few beers and a barbecued steak, the men sat on the veranda in the soft summer night and talked of the future. 'Here's the deal,' said Phil. 'We've been talking of this for a while. What we want from you, little brother, is for you to run our cropping and spraying programme, not as part of the management like us, but as a consultant agronomist. What do you think?'

Mike had been doing similar work in the south for several years by now. He liked the idea but didn't like giving up a nice safe government sinecure for the rough and tumble risk of private enterprise. But his brothers were sure they could muster enough clients for him. They offered seed capital for him to set up his office and their wives offered to find him a nice girl to keep his bed warm in the chilly winter. He accepted the proposal and the seed capital, but not the girl. He could find plenty of those for himself.

It worked wonderfully well. In two years, he had so many clients that he had two more agronomists working for him. A year later he purchased one of the big self-propelled spraying machines now appearing in the machinery yards and offered a crop spraying service. Five years later, with four sprayers and fifteen employees, he was making serious money.

Now, as he neared his forty-fifth year, he sat back to reassess his life. He had sufficient money, his health was good, but he needed something more in his life. He needed a companion, a soul mate, a lover.

Mike sold his businesses, invested the proceeds, and went to Europe for a year or so for travel experience and maybe a bit of adventure. He had always loved history, now he became part of it. He was not to know how adventurous it would be.

# MARIA ISABELLA MARTINEZ DE PALOMA

*Barcelona, Spain, 1995*

As a child, Maria had heard many stories of the fabulous wealth her ancestor had brought home from the New World four hundred and fifty years ago. There were tales of emeralds, silver and gold, and the legend of a magnificent statue of gold. Why then, she wondered, were they so poor?

She had grown up with her parents and brothers on a farm in Catalonia, about one hundred kilometres from Barcelona. They were not really poor, but she had always been told of the titled gentlemen who had been her ancestors, including the man who, they said, brought home the fabled gold statue, Sebastian Alfonzo de Martinez.

She always wondered about her ancestor, so many years ago, braving the oceans and hostile Indians to bring back treasure for Spain, and as she reached high school, she found herself more interested in history; she resolved to study it at the *Universidad de Barcelona*.

She talked it over with her father. Like many men, he loved his daughter very specially. He could deny her nothing, but this thing was not possible. He did not have the funds. Maria took this unwelcome news with equanimity.

She determined nothing would stand in her way, and in the New

Year, it rewarded her for her work with an all-expenses scholarship to attend the *Universidad*.

There she worked just as hard. She graduated with honours and got a post-graduate position with The *Universidad de Santiago de Compostela*. Once more, she excelled. Now she was ready to work even harder and study the history of Spanish America, maybe even to learn more about her ancestor's treasure. By 1995 she was in London, working at the British Museum in their Central and South American section. The world, it seemed, was her oyster.

But of course, her life had been more than endless study, although at times it seemed like it was not. She was a sociable girl and made many friends. She took part in several sports, but eschewed team and other competitive sports for those that provided a personal challenge, namely distance running and orienteering.

She had grown into a striking young woman with dark good looks, crowned by a face full of character, wide and depthless brown eyes, and long shining raven hair. As a result, she had many suitors, but she thought they were all a little puerile, and their attraction to her was mainly physical.

She preferred older men as companions, but she was still looking for a soul mate, someone she could love without reserve and who could return such a love, someone she could become as one with.

Now in her thirty-seventh year, she was a respected and well-known historian. Oxford University had offered her an associate professor's position in the History Faculty. She would begin there in the spring.

She had almost reached the pinnacle of her career; as far as that went, she was completely satisfied. She looked forward to the future; she had plans for worldwide research on several topics and the books she would write. But there was a void in her heart. She still lacked that single one in whom she could immerse herself and become as one with him.

Meanwhile, she looked forward to visiting her family in Barcelona, the warmth of the sun, and the lovely waters of the blue Mediterranean Sea.

# THE FORCES OF DARKNESS

*The Reischwald, Germany, 1995*

When *Obersturmbannführer* Rolo Giessner, now known as *Gefrieter* Heinrich Arner, waded across the small creek and surrendered to the Americans, he was bleeding badly from his self-inflicted wounds. After a cursory interrogation by the battalion intelligence officer, they transferred him to a field hospital and eventually to a military hospital in Hanover. They did not question his identity. The Allies had millions of German prisoners and displaced persons to process, and many SS and Gestapo slipped through the net. With the help of Nazi sympathisers in the Vatican, Geissner reached Rome, and sailed from Genoa to Paraguay.

They provided him with seed capital and over the years he built a small import business, bringing in machinery and parts from the USA for Paraguay's farmers. He never forgot his days in the SS and remained a fervent Nazi. But he was practical enough to know that the resurrection of the Reich was nothing but a pipe dream. He missed his homeland, of course, and he thought many times of the 'sacred' mission Himmler had given him to retrieve the golden eagle.

Now that he had capital enough, he waited until he adjudged it safe to return to Germany and he did so in 1980.

During his time in command of his *Einsatzgruppe*, he had extorted, by various means, many gold pieces and precious stones from the Jews, partisans and Russians who fell into his hands. It made sense to him; they would not need them where they were going, he might as well utilise them. He had concealed them in many places, chiefly in the west. Some were in East Germany, and he could not access them. He found some of his caches discovered, but most of his loot was still where he had put it over thirty-five years ago.

Giessner used some of his stolen riches to establish a prosperous BMW dealership. He dabbled in politics, always on the left, but this was merely camouflage. He had secret links to the neo-Nazis and began building a network. By 1985, he was ready to begin his search for Himmler's treasure. He had constructed a large country house in the *Reischwald* where he housed his henchmen with many layers of security and secrecy.

He started by seeking the Nazi records of the time. He described himself as a researcher, wanting to write a history of the SS, and he had access to most of the surviving records from the wreck of the SS headquarters at Prinz Albrechtstrasse 108.

One aid to researchers of World War Two is the dedication of the Germans to accurate and precise record keeping. The SS had been no exception. Giessner had plenty of material to work with, but these were mostly records of the *Waffen-SS*.

He was unaware at that time of the Potsdam records, and in any case, they were in East Germany.

In 1990, he looked at the Potsdam records, but he could discover nothing that revealed the ultimate location of the statue. He sent a team of his men to Paris. That was where most of the information pointed; it made sense as an operational headquarters.

By now Giessner was seventy-eight years old, but like many rich men, he could not get enough wealth. He wanted to gain that golden eagle before he died.

# THE GLIMMER OF GOLD

### Barcelona, Spain, 1995

Maria had a month to spend as she wished before she went to Oxford. She tried to find out more about her famous ancestor, Sebastian Alfonzo de Martinez.

She had learned much from her mother, but that was all hearsay. She had to find a verifiable paper trail. There was a surfeit of material on the era of the Conquistadors, and she was pleased to see Sebastian's name mentioned frequently in relation to the country now known as Colombia.

There were some ancient documents as well, shipping cargo and passenger manifests, lists of the treasures returned for the king, and some personal papers and journals of the men involved. After a week, she discovered a letter from Sebastian to his wife. It was banal, mostly personal news and protestations of love. But the last paragraph made her stir with excitement. It read:

'I bring with me for the greater glory of God and of Spain, a wonderful piece of the natives' work. It is a statue, in pure gold, of an eagle with remarkable emerald eyes. Do not worry, my dear wife, for this will relieve us of our debts and we will be rich once more.'

*So,* she thought, *this must be the treasure Madre spoke about. I wonder what happened to it.* She spoke to her mother again, showing her the letter. While her mother only had vague memories of the Martinez family, she knew that the line had died out. The last male had been unmarried. He had lived in a small house in Málaga, but they had not heard of him since the civil war, and she doubted he had survived. 'The communists held Málaga when the war started,' she said, 'with a name like that he would have been a marked man.'

Maria began a search of the property records of Málaga. She identified the location of the house, but it was long gone, destroyed in the war. Now a block of apartments occupied the site. By now she was getting sick of dead ends.

One evening, she saw on television a documentary about leading figures of the Civil War. The subject that evening was *Coronel* Luis Escardo. He had been at the battle for Málaga on the Nationalist side and his troops had taken the city. They had caused much damage by bombing and artillery fire and had ransacked the city for valuables at the same time. He had become a brutal military policeman and exemplified the terrible treatment of prisoners by both sides. No one had mourned him.

Maria wondered if the battle had destroyed the house and, if so, could the treasure have still been there? She followed the programme closely and learned that they had posted the *Coronel* to the Paris embassy. He had died there in mysterious circumstances. There were two women who talked about his strange disease and how he had raved about an eagle and a curse. Perhaps it might be a worthwhile line of enquiry.

She placed advertisements in the Paris newspapers requesting any information at all about *Coronel* Luis Escardo. The response surprised her. Several dealers in jewellery and precious metals contacted her about Escardo. All of them remembered their fathers and uncles speaking to a Spaniard about the value of gold and emeralds. They remembered him quite clearly, for he had described an emerald of such size that they disbelieved him. One said he seemed disturbed, maybe even a little mad.

## The Reischwald, Germany, 1995

Giessner received the phone call late in the evening. It was his chief in Paris calling to inform him that, in response to advertisements placed in that paper, *le Monde* had carried an article about a long-dead Spanish *Oberst* who had died in mysterious circumstances. There were several witnesses who said he had made enquiries about an enormous emerald.

Geissner's ears pricked up. Had not Himmler told him he had purchased the statue from a Spaniard?

Geissner had been around trouble all his life. He did not believe in coincidences. He ordered his men to find out who had been enquiring and to stand by for action when they knew.

A week later, he was told that they knew the identity of the enquirer. She was an academic who had just moved from Barcelona to Oxford in England. She was a Spanish national. Would it not be a clever idea to find out what she knew? He sent two men to England to question her. They were told to use whatever means were necessary to get her to talk. One of the men, Stavik, had been in Bosnia during that war; he loved interrogating women.

# AN ACCIDENTAL ROMANCE

*Oxford, England, 1995*

Mike Brodie made Ireland his first stop on his journey of discovery. He flew to London and changed for Dublin. In that fair city, he stayed for a week, doing all the things a tourist would do. He visited the old jail and was more than interested in the history of the British occupation, self-government and the nasty little civil war that followed. He took a train excursion to Cobh and visited the museum and the memorial to the Irish emigrants who had fled starvation and repression to the freedom of the world beyond.

He drove across the country to County Donegal in the far northwest of the Republic and spent a couple of days in the area from which his ancestor Brendan had migrated to Australia. It was interesting, but Mike gave thanks that Brendan had taken such a brave step; he much preferred the country around Brodie's Crossing. He spent a couple of evenings in bars, talking to the locals. The Irish love a friendly conversation, particularly when lubricated with several pints of Guinness. However, he found out nothing about the Brodies.

He took the ferry from Belfast to Stranraer in Scotland and worked his way south through England towards London. On the way, he fetched up in Oxford.

One of his school friends had won a scholarship to this august seat of learning and had returned with tales of the ancient buildings and habits of the students and faculties. He decided to stay for a few days. He spent most of his time walking the ancient streets. The old buildings, especially the colleges and the beautiful botanical gardens made a deep impression on him; in Australia, no building was much over two hundred years old.

On the last night in Oxford, he visited a small bar and drank some beer with the locals before he set off for his lodgings. It had begun to rain, misty rain that reduced the visibility to only fifty metres. He was just in sight of Magdalen Bridge when he saw a melee ahead. He hurried along the road; there was a young woman struggling with two hard-looking men. Mike came up short and called out, 'What are you doing? Let her go!'

One man was holding the woman by the shoulders, the other was trying to grab her by the legs. Behind them, a green car stood on the roadway, motor running, and the trunk lid open. It was obvious what was happening. Mike approached warily. The second man released her legs and stood up. '*Odjebi*,' he said, 'This is none of your business.' Mike stood his ground.

'If I were you, I would let her go,' he said, 'that is, unless she really wants to go with you.'

She turned pleading eyes on him. 'Please help me,' she said. 'I don't know these men.'

The man took a step towards Mike. 'If you value your life, you will go now. We have business with this woman. We will not hesitate to finish you.' Mike assessed the situation. They were near the bridge railing, and there were no cars around. His years in the army had taught him that surprise is always the best weapon of attack. He raised his hands submissively and moved to walk past the man. 'Okay, mate,' he said, 'She's all yours.'

He walked past him, pivoted and slammed his elbow into the side of his head. His target went tumbling over the bridge railing into the mass of punts moored below. Mike heard his surprised cry and the crash as he hit the boats, but his eyes never left the other one. Switched on now, back in that jungle again, ready for anything.

The first assailant hesitated, then he released the woman and produced a large knife. She screamed as he moved forward to meet Mike. He lunged with the knife, but Mike moved inside his thrust, grasped the arm and used the man's momentum to throw him aside. He hit the road surface hard and cannoned into the front of the car. Before he could get back fully to his feet, Mike kicked him hard in the side of his left knee, the one bearing the total weight of his body. He screamed and collapsed, ligaments badly torn, his kneecap dislocated. If ever he walked again, it would be with a stick.

Mike turned to the girl. 'Quickly,' he said. 'Into the car!' He ran to the rear and slammed the trunk lid closed, jumped into the driver's seat and sped away towards the town. He drove right through Oxford and into the countryside until he came to a roadside inn. He loved the names of English pubs. They called this one the 'Dog and Two Ducks'. He turned to the woman and said, 'That was a lot of fun. I think I need a drink. How about you?'

He looked across the car at her. He saw a handsome woman with beautiful dark eyes and a light milk coffee skin. She had a generous mouth and long, shining black hair. He thought she looked marvellous.

Maria looked at her rescuer and saw a fit-looking man of probably forty years. His hair must have been flaming red in his childhood but faded now and there were a few grey hairs there. He had nice grey eyes and a sardonic look on his face. *It is a face that has seen a lot*, she thought, *but is still full of life*. 'I think that may not be a bad idea,' she said. It was the start of something neither had ever imagined.

## The 'Dog and Two Ducks', Oxfordshire, England, 1995

The pub was built and decorated just like a dozen others Mike had sampled in the last few weeks. Lots of dark wood panelling, a riot of dogs and ducks outlined in stained glass, small tables with comfortable chairs. He led Maria to a corner booth and sat facing the door. He did not even think about it; it was a reflex action to sit with an unobstructed view of the door and his back to the wall near the rear exit. Once in Saigon, it had saved his life.

'Now,' he said, after he had found a pint of lager and a glass of wine, 'What was that all about? I would have bet you are good-looking enough to find a boyfriend in a more conventional way.'

The incident had shaken Maria, and she found his flippant remark of little comfort. Suddenly, she started shaking and tears began to run down her face. He saw her struggle to regain her composure and in a second, he was beside her, cradling her in his arms, nuzzling her hair and patting her shoulder. 'I'm sorry,' he said. 'My big mouth is always getting me into trouble.' Soon she calmed, but she remained in his arms; she felt warm and secure there, safe from her attackers. Slowly he disengaged, and she sat up, the beginnings of a shy smile coming to her lips. *God*, he thought. *When she smiles, she is so beautiful!*

Maria said, 'Thank you for your help on the bridge. They came out of nowhere; I had no time to react before they were upon me.' She spoke perfect English, but Mike knew she was not local. She had a faint foreign accent that made her voice extremely attractive, soft and musical to his ear.

'Well,' he said. 'They won't be troubling you again. Do you know who they were?'

'No, I have never seen them before in my life. I did not think I had such enemies anywhere, least of all in Oxford. I have only been here a few weeks. Perhaps they were common criminals looking for an easy mark.'

Mike reviewed the open trunk, the hard faces, the foreign accent and the knife. These were no ordinary muggers. They knew what they expected to do with her, or to her. He did not want to think about the latter. 'Well, let's forget about them for the time being. I don't even know your name. I'm Mike Brodie, all the way from Australia. You are from much closer, Italy perhaps?'

'Spain,' she said. 'I am a resident professor in history at the University. I am a historian. I am writing a book on the early conquistadors.'

'Amazing,' he replied. 'When I was a student, all the professors were pipe-smoking old men. If they had been as attractive as you, I would still be an undergraduate!'

She tried to hide a smile. She was relaxing. He was so easy to talk to, this warrior from the other side of the world. She wanted to stay with him, to get to know him better. Mike saw the smile and reached across to her, gently tilting up her chin. 'Keep smiling,' he said. 'You look beautiful when you do.'

She smiled again, a smile that seemed to come from deep within her. 'Thank you for being my knight in shining armour tonight. My name is Maria Isabella Martinez de Paloma, but you can call me Maria.' She smiled again, and there was a mischievous glint in her eyes. 'I don't know how to thank you properly. Are you in Oxford for a while?'

*Struth,* he thought. *I'll stay for as long as it takes!* 'I am on a tour of Europe, but I have a flexible itinerary. I am travelling alone at my pace, so I can stop anywhere if it takes my fancy.' *Or for anyone,* he thought. 'I have to go to London tomorrow, but I will come back in a few days to see you are okay.' Her dark beauty and her flashing eyes struck him. He would be back, alright, and the sooner the better.

'Tell me about yourself, White Knight,' she joked, 'I want to know everything about you, everything now, omit nothing.'

He found himself doing just that. It was so easy talking with her. He went through the pain of losing Anna, the treachery of Ricki, the hard year in Vietnam and his subsequent success in business, culminating in his early retirement and decision to see the world. He did not speak of the horrors of Vietnam, of the men he had killed or of the gallantry that resulted in his Military Cross. Mike was not a boastful man, and the war memories were for him alone, at least for now.

She listened quietly, reacting to his every word. When he told her of Anna, she reached out to cover his hand with hers. He felt a surge of excitement, a kind of buzz, a small electric shock. Only Anna had done that to him. Maria listened to him tell of his short and disastrous marriage, and she could feel his pain. She told of her life, of her famous ancestor, and of the fabulous treasure he had written about, how she had started a search for it herself. 'I do not want the money,' she said. 'I just want to know what happened.'

Mike understood. Many times, in his work, he had been confronted with problems that were inexplicable, that is, until his research and probing mind had uncovered an answer. There is nothing worse than trying to find an answer when there isn't one, and nothing so exciting as to be on its trail.

Maria felt herself being drawn to him, slowly but inexorably, into his being. She did not mind; she wanted to be part of him. *What is this feeling*, she mused. *Why am I so captivated by this man when I have rejected so many others?* She did not know why, but she was enjoying the experience. The landlord called for last drinks.

They gazed into each other's eyes and saw in each other something wonderful, inexplicable, comforting. Was this love, genuine love, unconditional love?

Mike broke the spell. 'I guess we better get going,' he said. 'It is late, and people will begin to wonder where you are. And I will have to dump the car as well, somewhere along the way.' Neither wanted to end the evening. They strolled slowly towards the car. In the dark interior, Mike could feel her presence, the warmth of her body, smell her soft and subtle scent, a mixture of sandalwood and something more exotic, a little dangerous, like a smouldering volcano waiting to erupt.

He drove her to the college and bid her good night. He planned to go to London in the morning but promised to return soon. She had work to do. He touched her hand and leant over and kissed her hair softly, drinking in her scent. Then he drove away. He left the car in a layby about a mile from the major highway and walked back to his hotel.

Maria walked up to her rooms; she was feeling like a schoolgirl again, thinking of boys, wondering, wondering, what it would be like. Maria had not felt like this, ever. She should not have let him go; she might never see him again. Oh, what a fool I am. I don't even know where he is staying. She slept fitfully.

### *The Reischwald, Germany, 1995*

Giessner had not received the daily phone call from England. This troubled him, because he thought it would be a simple matter for his two best men to snatch a mere girl from the streets of a sleepy English town.

He detested the English. They were so casual and disorganised. How had they ever won the war?

Just then, his aide knocked on the door. 'Ah, Siegfried,' he said, 'have our men reported from Oxford?' The man didn't answer, and instead handed him a sheet of paper. It was a typed report from the BBC wire service. It told of a strange incident in Oxford. A man had fallen from the Magdalen Bridge onto the boats below. He was dead. There was a large contusion on his left temple. They assumed he had struck his head on one of the punts. An ambulance had found and taken another man to hospital. He had a serious knee injury and could not walk. A large knife of foreign origin was on the roadway. The man refused to say anything to the police. Furthermore, a stolen car had been found a couple of miles away. Police said the incidents were almost certainly linked.

Giessner was furious. A simple task gone horribly wrong. God damn their stupidity! One was dead, the second could not be allowed to talk. He summoned Siegfried. 'Send Kurt over there and have him clean up this mess. Tell him to bring the woman if he can. And make sure the others know I will not tolerate failure.'

## London, England, 1995

Mike woke to a perfect summer day. It was sunny, with a few cotton-wool clouds drifting across the azure sky. From his hotel window, he could see the traffic on the Thames and the people scurrying across Waterloo bridge. As an Australian, even one of Irish extraction, this scene caused a stirring in his soul. Once this was the capital of the greatest empire the world had ever seen; there would never be another one like it.

As an Australian, and raised as part of that empire, he still felt a loyalty to this place. As an army officer, he had sworn an oath of allegiance to the Queen, and he was proud of his family's long involvement in British history.

Mike went down to breakfast and relaxed with the newspaper. He read the reports of the incident in Oxford two days ago with mixed feelings. The death of the man he had knocked off the bridge did not trouble him; that was just cleaning up vermin, but he thought once more about why the attack had taken place. There was something missing here. He hated unresolved problems, especially when it involved him, voluntarily or otherwise. He pondered it for a while, checked out, and set off in his hire car for Oxford.

## Oxford, England, 1995

Kurt had made a quick journey. He was on a flight to Manchester within a few hours, hired a car and set off for Oxford. Kurt was forty years old, and a committed neo-Nazi. He had learned his skills in the German army and later, on the streets, in the fights against the communists and socialists in the turmoil of the late sixties. He was a hardened criminal. Kurt did not think he would have much trouble with a woman. Perhaps he could have some fun with her as well. He could not understand Stavik's failure. He had never failed before.

Mike drove back to Oxford in a rising tide of excitement. He thought of Maria; she must know something. He wanted badly to see her, so badly that when he reached the hotel, he telephoned the college immediately. The lady who answered the phone sounded rather severe.

He could not remember Maria's convoluted name, so he asked for 'Maria, the Spanish lady professor.'

'Who are you?' she demanded.

'Tell her it is the White Knight,' he said. 'She'll want to talk to me, I'm sure.' After a series of clicks on the line, he heard her soft tones. 'Sir Mike,' she said, 'how lovely to hear your voice. Where are you?'

'I am back in Oxford at the Bell Hotel. I …'

'Don't move, I'm coming.' The phone clicked as she hung up. Twenty minutes later, there was a knock on his door. He opened it and stood there, gazing at an apparition of dark hair and flashing eyes. She came to him, and putting her arms around his neck, kissed him passionately. He fumbled behind her for the doorknob, picked her up and carried her to his bed.

## *Oxford General Hospital, England, 1995*

Kurt decided that the time to strike was during evening hours, with the wards crowded with visitors. He dared not ask for the target by name, since the police were probably keeping a watching brief, but guessed there would be no police presence in the hospital since the man was a victim, not a perpetrator, as far as they were concerned. Besides, he could hardly run away.

He had to hope that the man would be in a private room, not an open ward where it would be impossible to do anything. It took him about half an hour before he located the man, then he went down to the lobby and purchased a bunch of flowers for camouflage.

When he entered the room, the man looked up in surprise. 'Kurt,' he said. 'What are you doing here?' His eyes changed as fear overtook him; he knew extremely well what happened to failures in Giessner's shadowy world.

Kurt crossed the room swiftly and placed a hand over his mouth before he could call out. He slapped the man's damaged knee; pain would lessen his resistance. He pulled the hypodermic needle from his pocket and thrust it into his arm. It only took about thirty seconds to work. He left as quickly and as quietly as he had come. In the lobby, he passed two policemen just entering the hospital. Outside, he suppressed an urge to run towards the road where his car awaited. He drove off slowly into the night.

## *The Bell Hotel, Oxford, England, 1995*

They lay entwined, sated, as dusk fell across the town. Mike had never felt like this before, even with Anna. Maria seemed to him to be the most beautiful and exotic creature alive. They had made love with a passion that transcended all that had gone before. For her, the volcano had erupted. She had not known she was capable of what they had just done. She had found what she had been seeking all her life, but she had not known what it was until now. Eventually, they slept.

In the morning light, Mike rose on his elbow and looked down on the young woman beside him, at her beautiful face, her long raven hair falling across that sweet face, her perfect breasts, and her magnificent body. He too had found his dream, the woman who so gave herself that they now were as one. He knew he would love her forever.

She smiled up at him, and the smile went straight to his soul. '*Te quiero con todo mi cuerpo y alma,*' she whispered. '*Ámame siempre.*' He knew only a little Spanish, and he felt, rather than understood, much of what she was saying. He would soon learn that she would revert to her native tongue in moments of passion. Whatever it was, it sounded good to him.

He kissed her eyelids, her face, with gentle kisses that moved to her mouth. She reached for him, stroking his body gently, softly, until she reached the very heart of him. He kissed her breasts. And they came together again, as one, until the volcano erupted repeatedly. After, she said, 'Come *mi amor*, we will need breakfast if we are to continue like this!'

Downstairs, as they sat in the sun, they discovered they were famished. A mountain of eggs and toast later, they sat drinking coffee. It was a beautiful day. Mike felt he could sit here forever, just looking at her. She smiled again and almost caused his heart to stop. 'Dearest Maria,' he said, 'What are we to do now? How can we be apart?'

'I can take a little time,' she said. 'The students are not back for another six weeks. I will spend every second with you. Let me come with you to Europe. We can even visit my home near Barcelona. It is a beautiful place; you will enjoy it there. My family will welcome you.'

That decided, Mike broached the subject of her attempted abduction. 'That was no random event,' he said. 'Those men were professionals, and I suspect they were foreign. The one who spoke to me had an eastern European accent. Can you think why they were after you, anything at all? For example, could anything about your work be relevant?'

She sat deep in thought for a while. 'Perhaps my search for the golden statue has attracted someone who is also looking for it. I do not know where it went when it disappeared from the family house in Málaga, or even if it was ever there. The only documented evidence is the letter from the Conquistador and an account of an *Español Coronel* who died in Paris in 1940, raving about a golden eagle and a curse. I have identified him and found that he was in the battle for Málaga. It is possible that he may have found it and taken it to Paris.'

Mike considered this. 'In Paris in 1940, the Germans had control of everything. The Nazis plundered great works of art, jewellery, gold and whatever else took their fancy. I am sure that if they knew about this statue, they would have been keen to get their hands on it. Why don't we go to Paris? We may discover more about this colonel of yours.'

'I don't know,' she replied. 'Since the wall came down, there have been many German records made available from the East German archives. Besides, if it involved the Germans, there will certainly be comprehensive records. They wrote down almost everything. It would not surprise me if there were records of their daily bowel movements! Perhaps we should go to Berlin.'

They had given Kurt a good description of Maria, and he found a picture of her in a back copy of the Oxford Mail, in an article about some new members of the University faculties. He smiled to himself. *It might be fun to interrogate her,* he thought.

He walked the streets of Oxford, looking, looking. Near a small café, he may have seen her, but he was not sure, so after a while he hung about Magdalen College hoping for a sight of her. He wandered down to the bridge, wondering if this was the same one where Stavik had met his end. He looked over the railing and saw an area of boats closed off with police tapes. *So,* he thought. *How did the girl manage that?* Kurt cared little; he had never liked Stavik; he was an unfriendly, arrogant, Croat bastard.

He walked back along the street, by the botanical gardens, opposite the college. He was about to give up when a small hire car pulled into the kerb and a smart-looking, dark-haired woman stepped down and disappeared into the college. It was her! Now he would wait until she emerged and take her! He crossed the street and loitered along the side of the building, as if examining the stonework.

Mike had seen him cross the road in the rear-view mirror. The close-cropped blonde hair and the tattoos on his arms made him feel uneasy; the man looked most unlike a student or academic. He was big and looked more like a prize-fighter. *It might be prudent to keep an eye on him*, he thought.

Maria came out to the car. Mike noticed the big man look sharply at her and move towards her with a purposeful stride. He jumped from the car and ran to meet her, taking her in his arms and crying out, 'Julie, how good to see you!' He quickly took her to the car and they drove away. He could see the other man squinting at the car and writing something in a notebook.

'We make love all night and already you have forgotten my name!' she joked. 'What was all that about?'

'There was a bloke hanging about. He seemed a bit suspicious, so I tried to confuse him. Perhaps he was looking for you.'

'Oh, no! I hope he is not a friend of the others.'

'I think he might be,' said Mike. 'What we really need to do is speak with him. He may tell us what he knows.'

'Speak with him?'

'Yes, Vietnam taught me a little about extracting information. But first, we must set the trap. You are going to be the bait.'

'But, Mike, he may harm us.'

'I don't think so. I would never let anyone harm you, my darling. I want to do this to protect you. If this joker's what I think he is, he won't go away anytime soon, and we don't want him spoiling our honeymoon, do we?'

Kurt paused, frustrated. Who was the man she was with? He looked like the fellow she had been with at the café. Now he had a problem. Should he wait for her here? *No*, he thought, *she's carrying luggage. If she were to make an escape now, it would not please Giessner at all; perhaps I would become the next target of his wrath.* He ran down the street in the direction they had gone. With great relief, he saw a taxi rank and tumbled into a small green cab. 'Keep going down this road,' he said to the driver.

It rewarded him almost immediately. He spotted the car parked outside a row of shops, but before he could reach it, the man emerged from one shop and drove off. 'Follow that small blue Vauxhall,' he said to the driver. 'My wife is off with some cheating bastard. He is in for a surprise!'

The Vauxhall kept to a slow but steady pace through the town and into the countryside. Before long, it drew to a stop at a small country pub. "Ere you go, guv,' said the cab driver. 'Good luck.'

'Don't stop here! Drive on a little way.' About a mile down the road, they came to a fast-food restaurant. 'Stop here,' said Kurt. He waited until the cab disappeared into the distance and walked back the way he had come.

Mike and Maria entered the pub and asked for a room. When they settled in, they came downstairs for lunch. 'You're too late, love, lunch is over,' said the publican. 'But we can do you some sandwiches and coffee.'

Maria flashed those sparkling eyes at him. 'We would be very grateful,' she said. 'Could you bring them to us outside on the terrace?' They sat on the terrace in full view of the passing public. About a hundred yards away, Kurt crouched in the cover of a neighbouring farmer's hedge. He settled down to watch.

On the terrace, Maria said, 'It looks as though someone really wants to get hold of me. It must have something to do with the golden eagle.' She said, '*águila de oro*,' without thinking. 'I am sorry. I keep forgetting you do not understand Spanish.'

Mike looked at her. 'Anything you say is music to my ears, and as Spanish is a romance language, it is quite appropriate.'

She smiled that smile again. 'What are we to do now?'

'When we finish our lunch,' said Mike, 'we have to wait until dark. Can you think of anything you would like to do?' There was magic in her eyes.

'Yes,' she breathed, 'but first I would like to take a walk. It is such a lovely afternoon.' Kurt watched them walk away from the pub. It concerned him at first, but he realised they carried no luggage; they would be back. About two miles down the road, they stopped at a small village. It was not much, but Mike went into a post office store and emerged with two cold drinks and a copy of the Oxford Mail. He showed it to Maria. 'MYSTERY MAN DIES IN HOSPITAL' screamed the headline.

The story that followed left them in no doubt that this was the fellow Mike had maimed on the bridge. 'The plot thickens,' he said. 'This is too much of a coincidence. I'll bet our tattooed friend came here to clean up the mess the others made, and to finish their job for them.' They walked back to the 'Dog and Two Ducks'. In their room, they repeated the lovemaking they had enjoyed last night. This time it was slower, gentler and even sweeter. As dusk fell, they rose and made their preparations.

Kurt had risked a lunch break while his targets had taken their walk. Now he was back in his lying up position. Suddenly, he was wide awake. They had come to the door, arm in arm. He saw them kiss before the man waved to her and drove away. That was going to make it even easier.

Maria treated herself to a roast beef dinner and a glass of red wine, while the light leaked from the sky and a soft velvet cloak of darkness descended upon the quaint little pub. She monitored the other patrons while she sat. She saw no suspicious characters at all. They greeted each other cheerfully and seemed to know all but a few of the others. Regular patrons, no doubt. She waited. Time was on their side. Mike had spent many nights lying in wait on jungle trails for his quarry to arrive. Patience, he had learned, was a valuable skill. About eleven o'clock she made her move.

Kurt saw her come to the door, shrugging on a jacket. Now! Now I have her! He waited as she sauntered away towards the lights of Oxford, then he slithered from the hedge and followed about fifty yards behind her. He did not see the shadow detach itself from the rear wall of the pub and follow. The hunter had become the hunted.

Kurt watched the woman walk down the road towards the distant city. She seemed in no hurry. She stopped beside a small park and bent to retie her shoelaces, and she turned and walked off into the park, towards the trees and the darkness. Kurt was almost laughing with glee; she was making things too easy!

He quickly and soundlessly ran up behind her as she entered a copse of elms. But as he reached out to seize her, he felt a tremendous blow to his lower back. The pain from his kidneys was crippling, and he found himself flat on his face in the grass. Before he could rise, Mike drove both knees into his back as he leapt upon him. When he recovered, he found his ankles and wrists bound with multiple strands of insulating tape. Kurt was on his back. He could just make out a large figure standing over him; he was in acute pain.

'Now, you prick,' said Mike. 'What's this all about? What do you want with us?'

Kurt remained silent. 'Right,' said Mike. 'It looks as though you need a little encouragement to give us what we want. Do you enjoy women?' There was silence. Mike drew the large hunting knife he had purchased when he had stopped in the street. It glinted evilly in the faint moonlight. 'You know,' he said. 'I can fix it so that you never will again.'

The man spoke quickly in German. *'Ich spreche kein Englisch!'*

Maria said, 'He says he does not speak English.'

'Bullshit,' said Mike. 'He wouldn't come to England on this kind of job if he didn't. But if he speaks no English, I am sure I can get the message through with sign language.' He moved to Kurt and sliced open his clothing, exposing his genitals.

*'Nein, nein!* I will tell you what you want. Do not cut me.' Mike just smiled at him.

'You lied to me already; I think you will lie to me again. Perhaps I will remove an inch or so, just in case.'

It terrified Kurt. He babbled, pleaded and soon the truth poured out of him. He spoke for over five minutes. Maria took lots of notes. When he had finished, Mike shrugged his shoulders. 'I'm not convinced,' he said to Maria. 'I think I'll remove them just the same.'

Kurt screamed in terror. He soiled himself and began to weep. *'Nein, nein.'* He tried to roll over on his stomach, to conceal his vital organs. They left him there, whimpering, pleading for mercy.

There was a telephone booth on the other side of the park. Mike telephoned the Oxford Constabulary, and, speaking through his handkerchief, told them where they could find the man who had committed murder in their hospital. Early next morning, they drove to Manchester and boarded a flight to Berlin.

## The Reischwald, Germany, 1995

Siegfried took the latest news to his boss, filled with trepidation. Geissner almost exploded. *'Verdammte dummkopf!* Have I nothing but idiots to command? In the old days, I would have him shot.'

No one could tell him where the woman was, and how could she have defeated three of his men? He did not know what to do. If Kurt had told them anything, they would be in search of the statue again. He must assume that they knew everything. They will go to Paris, he calculated. She was there before; she knew about the Spanish *Oberst*, and she would try to follow it up. He decided to place his men at airports, ports and train stations. *This will use up all my men*, he realised. *But it is our best chance.*

## Berlin, Germany, 1995

It was still breakfast time in Berlin, so they left their scant luggage at their hotel and found a café for a second round of coffee. They had plenty of time, they reasoned. Nobody knew they were there. For the next two hours they played at being tourists.

They identified the building where the records were kept and the various museums containing World War Two material.

After lunch, they could gain access to their hotel room. Mike headed to the bathroom for a long soak. Maria went to the telephone. Thirty minutes later, she entered the bathroom. 'Is there room for me?' She smiled. Without waiting for a reply, she undressed. Mike watched in appreciation. She teased him, removing each item slowly, one at a time. *My God,* he thought. *She is so beautiful. How lucky I am!* They washed each other, kissing and fondling, until neither could wait any longer. They went laughing and still wet to the bed and made love, tenderly, more urgently, until the volcano erupted again.

Afterwards, she lay snuggled into his shoulder, and told him what she had learned on the telephone. At first, she had called her faculty head in Santiago. He had given her the name of a colleague in Berlin, a historian who knew his way around the Third Reich archives. She should have no problems searching all of them. Her academic status and her position at Oxford would open most doors.

They started immediately. Maria went to the archives and sent Mike to the museums, looking for any trace of a golden eagle. He found nothing. By then it was closing time and they met back at the hotel for dinner.

Maria had searched a lot of material entered into a computer database, but there was much still only available in old and dusty files. It was like looking for a needle in a haystack. Tomorrow they would both tackle this gargantuan task.

## National Archives, Berlin, 1995

They spent four days searching and found nothing. When they reported to their German friend, he said there were some records of the SS kept in a special depository in Bonn, former capital of West Germany. These were incomplete; they burned most of the records when Potsdam had been levelled by the bombing, the remains of these records discovered after re-unification and moved to Bonn, where suitable storage facilities existed. They would require special government permission to access them.

## Barcelona, Spain, 1995

Mike and Maria swam in the blue waters of the Mediterranean and lounged on the beach. He and Maria had lodged all the paperwork for permission to access the files in Bonn. They were told it might take two weeks or more to process their application. Maria was impatient, but Mike told her that the process in Germany was warp speed compared to Australia. In the meantime, they decided to holiday in Spain.

She had gone back to her research. She wanted to know more about the golden eagle. For a week she spent several hours a day in the museums of Barcelona. There was a wealth of information available, much of it hearsay from the sixteenth and seventeenth centuries, but she could not find much about eagle statues. She continued her search in Madrid. Besides the statue, there was a special exhibition concerning the Civil War. Maybe they could find out more about *Coronel* Escardo.

Mike went with her. He was experiencing the best time of his life. Every night was a fresh experience. He had awakened a passion in Maria she had not known was possible. She brought to him a mixture of gentle love and unrestrained emotion. She was like a wildcat when aroused. Their love had truly made them as one; few couples ever reached these heights.

## Madrid, Spain, 1995

In Madrid, deep in the bowels of the Biblioteca Nacional & Museo Arqueológico Nacional, she found what she wanted. The library had many books on the period and the museum had several Muisica gold pieces, some of which were effigies of the great Condors that were plentiful before the Conquistadors arrived. The natives crudely fashioned these pieces, and they bore no embellishments of precious stones, but they were evidence that this magnificent bird was important to the Muisicas.

She continued her search while Mike sought information about the *Coronel*. In the Civil War exhibition, with an English-speaking guide, he found references to the horrors visited upon prisoners by both sides. It named *Coronel* Escardo as the commandant of the prison in Madrid during the latter stages of the war, but there were no personal details. It was a dead end.

But on the second day, Maria struck pay dirt. In one book in the library, she discovered facsimiles of documents from the early sixteenth century. They comprised personal letters, reports from officials of the King, shipping manifests and personal journals. In the journal of a priest, she discovered a reference to the bird. It was a photocopy of a dirty piece of yellowed paper, much creased and handled, but it was clearly readable. She read it aloud to Mike.

'I report to you for the greater glory of God and of Spain, a heathen tale of one of the Muisica idols. This hath never been seen by Europeans, but it is sayeth that, in the City of Xanlata, the stronghold of the Muisica people the priests hold and protect it. It is sayeth to be an image of an eagle, cast in gold of great purity and containing precious stones, to wit, emeralds of immense value. It hath eyes that are small emeralds, facetted with such skill that they seem to move when light falls upon them. It is sayeth that no woman may set eyes upon it for she will immediately have her eyes struck out and become a slave for the use of any who so desireth her, and at the next full moon, the priests sacrifice her. These diabolical creatures teareth the hearts from their living victims and drinketh the blood from the still beating organ. Soon we will capture this accursed thing and eliminate such Devil worship, for the glory of God and of Spain.'

'Whew! These Muisica priests didn't muck around, did they?' Mike said. Maria turned to him with eyes alive with excitement.

'This is what my ancestor brought home from Colombia. This is the treasure that he wrote about. The *Coronel* must have found it in Málaga and taken it to Paris with him, but there is no mention here of a curse. We must go to Paris. That is where the eagle went. There must be someone who knows what happened to it. There are the people who replied to my advertisements. We could start with them!'

But fate was to change their course. The history professor in Berlin telephoned to say that their permissions to search the SS records in Bonn had been granted. On Monday, they could begin such a line of enquiry; Paris could wait. Maria phoned the airport and booked a flight for Sunday night. They had a weekend to fill in and they were truly like honeymooners for two days. Their passion continued to grow. They knew they would be together forever.

They wandered the old city and ate in magnificent restaurants. Mike found the delight of the tapas bars and enjoyed the Spanish beer. During the day, they roamed the green parks, often sharing a picnic lunch. And, all the time, their love grew as they developed little secret signs and touches. Mike was learning some Spanish, for she encouraged him to do so, and, as always, when she spoke to him of her love, she reverted to her mother tongue. He found it endearing, and he taught her some of the Australian dialect.

They made no plans. Both were too old for children and neither wanted to transport their lives to opposite sides of the globe. They were content to live in the moment.

# THE MISSING FILE

*Besonderen Aufzeichnungen, Bonn, Germany, 1995*

The Special Records Depository lies in the basement of a nondescript government building in the centre of the city. The building bears no signage or logo that would show its purpose, which was the storage and administration of sensitive government documents.

A security guard escorted Mike and Maria inside, their passports, documents and letter of permission subject to intense scrutiny before they went to the basement to the records storage. A severe-looking and senior police officer explained the conditions to them. 'Wear these cotton gloves at all times. You may not remove any of the documents. One of my officers will accompany you always. *Verstehst du?*'

'*Jawohl,*' replied Maria. 'We accept your conditions.' She turned to Mike. 'Let's get started, *mi amor.*' They followed their escort to the elevators. In the basement, they found a row of desks and several transparency readers. Requesting material accessed the records from the attendant.

They began. Mike found the documents impossible to read; he spoke no German. All he could do was check them against a list of keywords provided by Maria. She understood some written German, but the gothic script used on many of the documents made her task even harder. For two days, they searched and found nothing.

Late on the third day, Maria reached the bottom of one of the large boxes. She was tired, and her eyes and her head were aching, so she very nearly missed it. She called, 'Mike, come look at this!'

She bore in her hand a dark green folder. It was not as scuffed as some others, showing that it had little handling. There were the usual labels and folio numbers and dates written above the eagle and swastika motif of the third Reich, and below that was a title handwritten in large letters. It said:

## Der Steinadler

'*Der Steinadler*, the Golden Eagle,' breathed Maria.

They examined the file with great excitement. It was only a thin file, began in 1941, and it dated the last document in early 1945. But they could see that the file originated in the office of the *Reichsführer-SS* himself. They marked it with a designation that said in German:

### SECRET: FOR THE EYES OF THE REICHSFÜHRER-SS ONLY.

'This is it,' she said, 'this will tell us all that the Germans knew about the statue, I'm sure.' Maria turned to the policewoman who had accompanied them to the basement and tried to speak with her, but the officer spoke only limited English and Maria's limited German was inadequate for this purpose. She took Maria to the reception area, where she asked if it would be possible to arrange an English or Spanish translation of the file's contents. She was told she could collect it the next afternoon. 'Come,' she said to Mike, 'let us go to the hotel now. I need a rest and a long hot bath.'

That evening, they decided to have a celebration of their successful search. They had returned to the hotel and spent half an hour in a foaming spa bath. For Mike, it was as if he had died and gone to heaven. He lay there, feeling the tiredness and tension of the last few days seep away and his muscles become relaxed and soft as though he was cooked pasta. Maria soaped and washed him. He looked at her perfection through half-closed eyes and thanked whoever was responsible for bringing them together.

They took turns with the washcloth until they felt the magic rising. She led him to the bed. He felt so good, so good, as he stroked her, kissed her, found her special places. *¡Dios mío!* She wanted him so badly. She opened herself to him, to his gentle hands, to his hard body. '*Te quiero*, Mike, *mi amor por siempre*,' she cried as her orgasm surged through her. She had never been so happy.

Mike could not believe his good fortune. *I expected nothing like this*, he thought. *Thank God she has come into my life.*

As the light faded from the sky and the magic lights of the city came on, they rose and prepared to spend a night on the town. Neither had been in Bonn before, so they sought information from the hotel staff. Mike told them he had only just met the woman of his dreams. Where should they go tonight? The advice was plentiful, especially from the females, excited in the feminine way about love affairs. The men were mostly thinking about what they would give to be in Mike's shoes this night. After much discussion, they set off into the evening.

They started with a cab ride to the Nordstadt district, to the Cafe Pawlow, on the *Heerstraße*, for beer and bratwurst. The café was pulsating with life, putting them in the mood for a memorable night. Mike was a beer drinker by preference, and he had his favourite Australian beer, but he really liked to try different beers. He had come to the right place.

After that, it was back in a cab again and on to the *Martinsplatz* and the Roses Restaurant. 'Maria,' he said, 'This is perfect!' The restaurant was a stark contrast to the Cafe Pawlow, with muted lighting, private tables and the sound of soft music. On the way in, they presented Maria with a blood-red rose, the signature service of the establishment. The waiters seemed to know that they were lovers and provided a very discreet yet attentive service. Mike asked if they could sample a few German dishes since they had not been to Germany before and left it to their imagination. It was superb, especially the Schnitzel. After the food they were replete. Maria gazed across the table at her man. She took his hand. 'Mike,' she said, 'this is so lovely, so appropriate. I love you with all my heart. I will never leave you. You must be with me forever.'

He felt the same. 'We are one now, we are indivisible. Wherever we are, I am yours and you are mine.'

They toasted their love with a soft and slightly sweet Rhine valley wine. Then they set off for the hotel. Their night was only just beginning. In the morning, they stayed in bed for yet another bout of lovemaking before setting out for an early lunch. They were bursting with anticipation to read the file. The Germans are nothing if not thorough. They provided copies in both English and Spanish, rewarded with a million-dollar smile from Maria.

Mike said, 'As long as I have you beside me, I will have every request granted. Have you any idea how beautiful you are?' She smiled but said nothing.

Relaxing with large cups of coffee in the Stadtgarten, with a view of the Rhine, they began to read, with mounting excitement, the story of Himmler's affaire de cœur with the golden eagle. They learned of how he had purchased it from a Spanish *Coronel* in Paris, how that man had appeared to be sick or mad or both, how Himmler's emissary had stolen the statue, killed a guard, and tried to take it to Switzerland, only to die with his lover in a train crash.

They read of the French fireman who had found it and took it to Switzerland at the cost of his own life, and how two Abwehr agents had recovered it. They had found one dead in the railway car, the other had disappeared, somewhere between Dijon and Paris.

The trail had gone cold there. Himmler sent one of his best men to search, but he was unsuccessful. Eventually, they recalled *Obersturmbannführer* Rolo Giessner. The war was becoming desperate, all able-bodied men needed at the front. That was where the file ended, in April 1945. The war in Europe was almost over. Himmler would never have his golden eagle, but where was it?

# OCCASIONAL DETECTIVES

### Bonn, Germany, 1995

Maria did not want to leave Germany without an attempt to find out what they could about Rolo Giessner. He was the last man to be involved in the hunt for the statue; he may have recorded some vital information. In the morning, it was back in the archives. This time they were lucky. They found the information after an hour in the basement. They listened with great interest as the attendant translated for them.

Rolo Giessner had been a Nazi almost from birth. He had a lengthy career in the *Hitler-Jugend*, the SA, and the SS. In 1940, he had been responsible for the murder of a group of British prisoners, whom he forced into a barn which he set on fire. His men stood around the building and shot down any who got out. But his career became even darker after the German invasion of Russia. He had commanded an *Einsatzgruppe*, a murder squad that followed the army into Poland and Russia, killing thousands of Jews. He disappeared on the Russian front in April 1945, never seen again. The file had no photograph of the man. It looked as though they had gotten as much as they were going to get. So, where to next? The assistant suggested they should contact the Simon Wiesenthal Centre's Paris office; *they* might have some more information.

They took an overnight train to Paris. The trains in Europe are fast and comfortable. Maria had arranged a sleeper compartment, so they had a comfortable trip snuggled together. 'We could have taken a flight,' she said, 'but we would not save much time, and besides, we have this time to ourselves. The sleep will do us good.'

The sleep ended in an early morning lovemaking session, and they were ready for anything when they arrived in the French capital. Mike hailed a taxi, and they set off for their hotel. Neither noticed the man wearing a green t-shirt who ran to the taxi rank behind them.

## The Reischwald, Germany, 1995

*At last*, thought Geissner. *Some encouraging news.* He had been about to give up on his Paris vigil when the call came through. The woman had arrived in the city by train. A man who was unknown to them accompanied her.

It did not matter; his men could deal with him. It was important to find out what they knew. Now he would have his opportunity to do so. He made his dispositions. The entire Paris group would keep a twenty-four-hour watch on the couple. It might be a clever idea to give them a little rope in case they found out more.

Then they would take them to the safe house for interrogation. Also, Giessner wanted to find out what had happened to his three men. They were some of his best and he could ill afford their loss. He called in his aide and ordered his aircraft to be readied. He would fly to Paris in the morning.

## Simon Wiesenthal Centre, Paris, France, 1995

A slim, efficient-looking woman in her late sixties met them at The Simon Wiesenthal Centre's front desk. She welcomed them to her office and asked what she could do for them.

Maria said, '*Bonjour* Madame. *Que vous parlez anglais?*'

'*Oui*, how may I help?'

Maria explained that she wanted to find out more about

Obersturmbannführer Rolo Giessner. She explained that she had seen his SS file, but it was incomplete. Crucially, there was no photograph. The woman picked up the telephone and rattled off a conversation in rapid French. Then she said, 'Raoul may be able to help you. Please take a seat, he should not be long.'

A few minutes later, a slim man of about thirty-five years appeared and ushered them into his office. 'I am a researcher for the centre,' he explained. 'I work mainly in exposing ex-Nazis who escaped retribution after the war. Various organisations helped many to flee abroad, particularly to South America. Later, believing themselves safe to do so, some returned to Germany and other European countries to resume life under an assumed identity.'

'Giessner is one who we believe has returned. So far, we could not uncover him. We think he is in Germany, and we assume he is using a false name, but we know only that.' Raoul continued to outline Giessner's brutal career, but he had no more information than that provided by the file in Bonn. 'But,' he said. 'We have a photograph that you are welcome to.'

Maria and Mike were excited by that. Maybe they would at least know what their hunter looked like. Raoul led them past a display of memorabilia of the resistance. There were weapons, maps, photographs and other things. Mike was a farm boy, exposed to firearms at an early stage and in his army days; he looked closer at the display.

Raoul said, 'You can examine those later. It is a private collection belonging to Ruth, our receptionist. She was a member of the Resistance.' He took them into a sterile archive storage area, where he switched on a computer and began a search. He soon had the information on Giessner on the screen. There was a photo of him in his SS uniform, a thin-faced, bitter-looking man with a scar on his neck. 'I will print out what we have, and you can take it with you,' he said, 'and perhaps we can do something with this photo.'

He selected the photo and saved it. Then he opened another program and copied the photo to it. 'With this software,' he said, 'we can manipulate the photograph. I can try to age it so that we may have some idea of what he might look like now.' He manoeuvred the mouse and clicked on several buttons. 'How old would he be now?' he asked.

Maria did a quick calculation. 'Late in his seventies, I think. He would have been at least seventy-five.'

'Okay, I will do two images, one as if he has aged normally and one as if he has grown fat on his ill-gotten gains.'

They watched as the images redrew. As if by magic, the face changed, but it was clear that it was the same man. 'The eyes,' said Raoul. 'You cannot change the eyes, except for the colour, with contact lenses. The shape remains the same, and the location in the skull.' They took the images and the printouts and returned to the reception area. 'Ruth,' said Raoul, 'our guests would like to have you run through your little collection for them. *S'il vous plaît.*'

Ruth was pleased to do that. She opened the glass doors of the cabinet so that they could get a better view. Mike asked, 'That pistol, is it a Walther?' Ruth shook her head. 'It is a Luger,' she said. 'Would you like to have a closer look? It is rather special.' She took it from the cabinet and handed it to Mike. It was an ornate version of the usually utilitarian models the Wehrmacht issued.

It had carefully carved grips with a shield or coat of arms; on the receiver there were words engraved in German. '*Für Hans, lieben von der Mutter*'. Mike felt a little jar in his brain.

'What do these markings mean?' he asked.

'When the war came, their parents or girlfriends gave many of these pistols to the young soldiers. The carving is probably a family coat of arms, or the arms of the city they came from. Here, the engraving says, in English "For Hans Love from Mother".'

Maria looked at him. 'Hans? Can that just be a coincidence?' She turned to Ruth. 'Can you remember where you got this?'

'As clearly as yesterday. I do not have time now to explain. Can you meet me at ten in the café across the road? It is Le Café Monique. I will have my coffee break and I will tell you all I know then.'

They sat in the park nearby and talked about their progress. 'If the "Hans" on the pistol is the Hans Langer mentioned in the file, it will be unbelievable. Can you imagine how many "Hans" there are in the whole of Germany?'

Maria said, 'I don't think we will get much more information here. It would be too good to be true.'

Mike said, 'It may be better than you think. In intelligence gathering, every little bit of information may be important in eventually completing the jigsaw. Let's wait and see.' He put his arms about her and they were like young lovers again. I imagined after Anna and Ricki my life would be empty, he mused. Now it is overflowing! Neither saw the tall blonde man watching them from the shade of some trees on the far side of the park.

In the café, they settled over their coffee, and Ruth began her story. 'I was only a girl when the Germans came,' she said. 'They killed my father early in the war. Later, they came for my family. My older brother and I escaped because we had loitered on the way home from school. We never saw our mother and the little ones again. A neighbour took us in. I was only fifteen, Seth seventeen. It was not safe to stay there, so we left the city and took refuge on a farm in the Bourgogne for a while before we joined the Marquisards in the forests. We travelled to the Jura, to a hideout.'

'In the early spring of 1944, a patrol of us came upon a small survival hut, built in the mountains for skiers who become lost or need shelter from blizzards. There we found a man near to death, emaciated, with long hair and beard, and he seemed to be out of his mind. He kept muttering some names. "Helga" was one of them. Also, he talked of a "golden eagle". We thought nothing of it. He was German, and we knew he was a deserter. We took him back to our encampment, but he died soon after. Just before he died, he seemed to become more lucid, and he convulsed and cried out, "Der Steinadler ist es mir!" I knew a little German. I was sure he was saying "the golden eagle is mine" but we dismissed it as the ravings of a dying man. We buried him there, and I took his Luger, the one in my collection. It is a good pistol, I despatched several Boche with it.'

Ruth suddenly noticed that both her visitors were staring at her, opened mouthed in amazement. 'Is there something wrong? Are you alright?'

'There is nothing wrong, Ruth, but you may have solved an ancient riddle for us. Do you think you could tell us exactly where this hut was located?'

'I am not sure. The topographical maps may show it. If not, there are special maps for skiers. You might find one in a ski shop or an outdoors supplier. If you find one, bring it back and I will try to identify it for you.'

No one had noticed the tall blonde man at a nearby table. As soon as they left, he abandoned his cake and coffee and rushed from the café.

It took them a couple of hours to find what they wanted, and after lunch they returned to the Simon Wiesenthal Centre. Ruth took a while to find the hut, but finally identified one in the mountains above the town of Morteaux.

'Thank you so much. We will return to see you when our business in France finishes,' said Maria. 'Merci beaucoup, we must go now.' After they had left, Ruth picked up the telephone and placed an international call.

### Hotel Tour Eiffel, Paris, 1995

'Tonight,' said Maria, 'we have more to celebrate. A nice dinner would be lovely before we leave Paris.'

'Just what I was thinking,' Mike replied, 'and a walk along the river in the moonlight. Then home to sleep unless you can think of anything else to do.'

There was a mischievous glint in her brown eyes. 'I suppose we could watch television.'

'I think there is another vision I want to watch,' he said. 'A vision of satin and lace and a beautiful woman. I would like to interact with her. Do you know anybody like that?' She just smiled.

Outside, the tall blonde man had gone, replaced by another hard-looking man with dark hair. The blonde man had taken a Metro ride to an outer suburb. There he was meeting with an older man.

## *238 Rue de Vincent, Paris, 1995*

They set the safe house back about fifty metres from the street frontage. The house blocks were larger than normal. This was an old suburb, once popular with rich businessmen, now a little faded. They had divided most of the large houses into apartments; this one had not been touched.

Geissner sat in the sitting room on the ground floor, listening to the tall blonde man report on the day's activities. He covered the movements of the Spanish woman and her companion as they visited the Wiesenthal Centre and the subsequent conversation partly overheard in the café.

The man, named Otto, said, 'I could not hear it all, but the Jew bitch was telling them about her part in the war. She told them she found a Luger, and they all became excited, and the young woman said that it solved their problem. Later, they took what looked like maps back to the office. Perhaps they were looking for a particular place.'

'Well done, Otto. We must keep them in our sights and be ready to follow wherever they go. You are to collect Markus and go to the aircraft. You know where we store the weapons. Use your diplomatic passport to remove them and both of you report back to me. Meanwhile, it might be instructive to visit the old Jewess. She will tell us what she knows, I'm sure.'

Geissner sat thinking about this latest information. What if the couple had discovered the whereabouts of the eagle? Maybe it would be better to leave them alone for now. If he had them followed, they might lead his men to the treasure. If they did not, he could always have them snatched later. They must follow them as far as they went. That would use up three of his men. The old Jewess would only need one to squeeze the information out of her.

Finally, they could do to her what they should have done fifty years ago. '*Mien Gott,*' he swore. '*Der Führer* was correct. The *verdammte Juden* are still causing trouble! Well, tonight we will rid the world of one more!'

## Le Pont Neuf, Paris, 1995

Mike wanted to have one more conversation with Ruth. He had been thinking of the last words of the Abwehr agent whose pistol she had discovered. Maria suggested they telephone her.

'Can you come to my apartment after you have dinner?' said Ruth. 'I am sure I may remember more if we talk long enough.' They agreed to do that.

They failed to see the dark-haired man follow them to the restaurant, climbing from his taxi as they entered. He, in turn, did not notice the young man following him. If he had, he would have noticed the man's Mediterranean features, with thick black hair and moustache. He looked like a Greek or Iraqi.

The first man, known as Graf, hurried to a nearby telephone. His first ring was answered by Giessner. 'I have them in a restaurant near the *Pont Neuf*,' he said. 'What now?'

'Stay with them. Do not lose them under any circumstances.'

Mike and Maria had a most enjoyable dinner, after which they set out on their walk along the river. At the *Pont Neuf*, Mike leant over to her and said, 'Don't look back, but there is a man behind us. I am sure I saw him in the hotel lobby earlier. I think he has been following us. Stop in the middle of the bridge and pretend you are kissing me.'

'Pretend? I can do better than that!'

When they reached the centre of the bridge, Mike took her in his arms. There was no doubt about it; she was not pretending. He manoeuvred her to the side of the bridge so he could look back down the thoroughfare, but the man had gone.

## 1217 Rue des Soldats, Paris, 1995

Ruth's apartment was on the second floor. They could hear light classical music and there were many lights on. There was no elevator, so they climbed to the second floor to #7, her apartment. Mike reached out to knock, then stopped. The door was partly open.

He looked at Maria. She shrugged her shoulders. Motioning her to stay on the landing, he stealthily pushed the door open. There, on a chair in the kitchen sat Ruth, bound to the chair with duct tape and her dress torn open down to her waist. A squat, fair-haired man was leaning over her, about to force a glowing cigarette to her chest.

Mike crossed the room in one bound and delivered a savage punch to the base of his skull. The cigarette went flying, and the man dropped like someone had shot him. He did not move.

Maria had now entered the apartment. She went quickly to the kitchen counter and found a sharp knife, cut Ruth loose and covered her with her torn clothing, holding her while she regained her composure. 'Are you alright?' she asked.

'I am now, thanks to you,' she replied. 'They did much worse to me in the war. I should not have been taken by surprise. I must be getting old.'

Maria took her to her bedroom to find some new clothes. Mike turned to look at the man on the floor. He rolled him over to expose a flat and ugly face, much pitted by acne or something worse. He was still breathing but drawing shallow and ragged breaths. Mike felt in his throat for a pulse; it was faint but regular. The man would live.

The women had returned by now, and together they turned out the assailant's pockets. They found nothing that showed who he was, no passport, no wallet, nothing but a small notebook and pencil, and some small denomination banknotes and loose change.

Inside the notebook, they found all the entries were in German. There was what looked like a list of times and places. The places were cafes, the Simon Wiesenthal Centre and Ruth's address. It appeared that he had been following her since they had been at her office. 'This mongrel has been following you, Ruth,' he said. 'What do you think this means? I am sure they have followed us too. Is it connected; do you think?'

Ruth said, 'Almost certainly. This man is a German. Take off his coat and shirt.' When they exposed his upper body, they could see a swastika tattoo on his upper arm. 'A neo-Nazi,' she said.

Maria looked to Mike. 'I think it is time to tell Ruth just what we are searching for,' she said. 'Our visit to her has put her in danger. She should know what to expect now.'

'I know always that these animals are still out there,' she said, 'but I cannot let them disrupt my life. I have had such experiences before and I have managed to either handle them or avoid them, but this one caught me unprepared. I was expecting you, and I opened the door without thinking.'

'Well,' said Maria, 'let's sit down and we will tell you all we know.'

'First,' said Ruth, 'I will make some coffee. I am quite addicted to it. It was sheer torture during the war when it was so scarce!'

They told her of the golden eagle, of the SS brute Giessner and how Himmler had been possessed by a desire to retrieve the statue. They told of the two Abwehr agents who were the last known to have possession of the eagle. 'That is why we were so excited by the pistol,' said Maria. 'Hans Langer was the agent who disappeared, along with the golden eagle. We think he concealed it near the hut where you found him.'

'Now I understand his ravings,' said Ruth. 'He was still trying to establish his ownership as he died. It must be a precious thing.'

Mike said, 'We believe they cast it from almost pure gold, and it contains some valuable emeralds as well.' He continued. 'I think we may connect these goons we have encountered to Giessner. Why else would they be following us? They must know now we are hot on the trail.'

'Wait a minute,' said Maria. 'I remember noticing a tall blonde man in that park where we read the Giessner file. There was a similar man near us in *Le Café Monique*. Now that I think about it, I am almost sure that it was the same man. He could have overheard our conversation.'

'*Oui,*' said Ruth. 'If he did, he would know we may have solved the problem. That is why this one came here. He wanted to know what I knew.'

'What did he say to you?' said Maria.

'He had no time to ask anything. He said he wanted information, and he was going to show what he would do if I did not answer him. Then you arrived.'

Mike had been sifting through the notebook. Inside the back cover there was a telephone number, heavily underlined. 'Is this a Paris number?' he said, showing it to Ruth. '*Oui,*' she said, 'it is an older suburb on the outskirts of the city proper. It was once fashionable, but now run down, large houses split into student apartments. Some of the big old houses remain in their original condition.'

Mike looked pensive. He said, 'Maybe exactly right for a hideaway. Big house, extensive gardens, away from the road and neighbours. It seems ideal. I think I will try that telephone number.'

He dialled. The phone answered almost immediately. '*Konrad, was haben Sie entdeckt? Was hat die alto Jüdin kennen?*' The voice was that of an old man, impatient, querulous, demanding. Mike did not answer. '*Wer ist dass?*'

Mike hung up. The others had listened, close to the handpiece. Ruth said, 'Perhaps he was expecting a call from our friend here. He said something like "what did you find out, what did the old Jewess know?"'

'Could it have been Geissner?' said Maria.

Ruth said, 'I would bet on it. I have heard that kind of voice before. He is used to instant obedience, he is arrogant, impatient and he wants answers right now. The SS were all like that.'

'Well, we know what is happening now. We are being followed by Geissner's men. He wants the golden eagle. We must go to the Jura. The answer will be there. But we will have to make sure we have proper equipment and are ready for anything.' said Mike.

'I will come too,' said Ruth. She held up her hand. 'Yes, I am not young, but I am not dead yet, *and* I know the area, I know the mountains, and I know where to look. Tomorrow we will prepare.'

Maria said, 'What are we to do with this *sucio animal?*'

'Leave him to me,' said Mike. 'We will leave now.'

Mike picked up Konrad in a fireman's lift and carried him down the stairs and along the street for a hundred metres and dumped him in an alley behind a row of dark and shuttered shops. They continued down the street and found an open bistro where Maria telephoned for a cab. They had not noticed the young man of Mediterranean appearance who watched them leave Ruth's apartment.

## 238 Rue de Vincent, Paris, 1995

Graf had not returned to the house since he had made the phone call from *Le Pont Neuf* hours ago, and now there was this telephone call. Geissner was deeply disturbed. Who could have accessed this telephone? It was an unlisted number, used only by his men to report to him. It was never used to make calls. Only the few men he had in the field used it.

He waited for Konrad to report, but the call did not come. Had the *dreckigen Jude hure* overpowered Konrad and found his number? *Nein*, it was not possible. What had happened? He heard the door open and realised that Otto had returned. Otto and his companion had encountered no difficulties with French Customs. They entered carrying a box containing several Glock17 9mm pistols, a H&K MP7A1 4.6mm submachine gun and ammunition. Now they were ready for the chase and the capture of the golden eagle. Konrad did not telephone.

In the morning, they heard on the radio news that a man matching Konrad's description had been discovered in the Seine downstream from the city. He had a broken neck. The police had not ruled out foul play. Now Giessner really worried. He had lost three men in England, and now Konrad was dead, and Graf was missing. He had to force this thing to a conclusion, and soon!

## 1217 Rue des Soldats, Paris, 1995

They met early at Ruth's apartment and began to put together a shopping list. There were many items to buy. They needed suitable clothing and decided on army surplus pants and boots.

They each needed an anorak for, even in summer, the temperature could fall rapidly on the mountains, especially at night. They purchased a cooking pot, boxes of MRE (Meals Ready to Eat), waterproof matches and torches with spare batteries.

They needed maps, a compass and a protractor for their navigation, sunglasses, nylon ropes and carabineers, and hats. Finally, they would need small light collapsible tents, and roll up, ultra-light raincoats.

They divided the tasks between themselves and set out on a mini shopping spree. By late afternoon, they were ready. In the morning, they would pick up a rented Land Rover and set off on their journey. Earlier, Maria and Mike had checked out of their hotel; they intended to spend the night in Ruth's apartment. Since the incident of the night before, Mike's jungle-trained senses had shown that their tail might not be done with his activity. He did not want whoever it was to pick them up at their hotel again.

The next day they set out. Ruth had surprised them as they loaded the Land Rover by producing another pistol, a US army Colt 1911A that she had brought home from the war, as well as a .22 sporting rifle. 'Don't worry,' she said, 'I have licenses for them both. I have a feeling that we may need them.'

## 238 Rue de Vincent, Paris, 1995

Giessner had called a council of war. He now had only three men left he could count on. It tempted him to go with them but decided not to. They would need a base and someone to act as a control centre.

He had Otto watch the apartment on *Rue des Soldats* one last time. Otto found the street empty except for a group of boys kicking a football around on the sidewalk. He went to the door of apartment #7 and knocked. There was no answer. Looking furtively around, he withdrew a set of skeleton keys and let himself in.

There was nobody inside. He could sense the stillness as soon as he went through the door. He made a careful search, room by room. There was nothing to show where they had gone except a scrawled shopping list on the kitchen table; they had been looking for camping equipment, it seems. He went back down to the street, where the boys were still playing with their football. He went over to them. 'Did you boys see anybody around number 1217?' he asked.

One boy said that there had been a 'cool-looking' Land Rover there earlier. 'It looked like one of those new ones with the diesel engine,' he said. 'I'd really like to go camping in one of those! It was bright red and had a spare wheel on the back door, just like an African safari.'

'Did you see who was driving it?'

'There was a tall man driving, and two women, or perhaps one woman and one man, it was hard to tell the one in the back. The windows were dark.'

Otto handed him a 10 Franc bill. 'Anything else? Did you see the plates?'

'It looked brand new. Maybe it was a hire car because there were labels on the back windows, and the license plate had a double "B". That's all I know. Thanks, mister.'

Otto phoned the safe house and relayed the information to Giessner. 'Excellent work,' he said, 'return here.' When Otto returned, he joined the meeting. For once, Giessner could not decide. After an hour of to-ing and fro-ing, with no progress in the debate, he decided. 'The *Abwehr* agent Hans Langer disappeared from the train somewhere at or near Dijon,' he said. 'You must go there. It will be the best place to start. I will remain here and direct the operation. You must find them; you must recover *der Steinadler!*'

Otto, Markus and the third man, Gerd, loaded the weapons and equipment into a small blue Mercedes before changing into sturdy work clothes. They were about to leave when Giessner called them to the sitting room and gestured wordlessly at the television. Otto was the only one who understood French well, but the pictures told the story. Emergency workers were lifting a body from a large rubbish skip. They only got a glimpse of the face, but there was no doubt that it was that of Graf's.

The announcer said that his throat had been cut. It was the second such incident in as many days. Neither victim had carried identification of any kind, except a swastika tattoo. Police speculated it could be the beginning of a gang war. Giessner was terrible in his rage. The others quailed before him. He began to rant, walking backwards and forwards, sometimes raising his right arm. Otto remembered old newsreels of *der Führer*. Finally, he turned to face them, his eyes staring, spittle on his chin and his face as red as a ripe tomato. *Mein Gott, er ist wahnsinnigen*, thought Otto. *The statue has unhinged him!*

The trio left in a hurry. It was a long drive to Dijon. As they sped away, a small grey Opel sedan pulled out from the kerb about a hundred metres away and followed them.

### *Near Auxere, France 1995*

They had made good time. The Land Rover surprised Mike with its performance. It cruised easily at 110 km/hr. and rode comfortably, thanks to its supple coil springs. It was nothing like the army Land Rovers he had travelled in so long ago. He had been watching a small silver Renault in his mirrors. It had been behind them for some time now. His intuition told him it might be following them; his logic told him that this was a major highway and there were many thousands of small silver Renaults in France. He decided to put it to the test.

Up ahead was a rest stop. He indicated he was about to turn right into the parking lot, took the turn, and stopped. The silver Renault rushed by without hesitation. Mike could see nothing of the driver, except that it was a man. In the next five minutes, two more identical silver Renaults passed by.

'Is there a problem, darling?' asked Maria. 'Why did you stop?'

'I thought we might be being tailed,' he said. 'But now I don't think so. How about coffee and a change of driver?'

Soon they were on their way again, Ruth in the driver's seat. She drove with the natural confidence she had shown with everything she had done. Her days with the Marquisards had done that to her.

They stopped for the night in the town of Nuits-Saint-Georges. Tomorrow they would be in Morteaux. Maria was especially affectionate this night. She made love to him with all her fiery Spanish passion. Both had never felt so close to each other. They were as one now. Nothing could change that.

'Maria,' he said, 'What are we going to do with this thing if we find it? It must be worth many millions. We do not have the right to have such money. In any case, how could we spend it?'

She replied, 'The eagle has brought much pain and suffering to so many. Perhaps we could use the money for good. There are many places around the world that need basic things like water, schools and medicine.'

'Yes, I know,' he said, 'but who really owns it? Should it not go to its rightful owners?'

'The original owners are long gone. If we give it to Colombia, it will probably end up in some dictator's Swiss bank account. Maybe the Spanish government could take possession and sort it out via diplomatic means.'

He fondled her again, her beautiful skin, her secret pleasure centre. 'Let us not worry now,' he said. 'We may never find it.' She kissed him and ran her hands down his chest. ¡*Dios!* She wanted him so much! '*Hazme el amor mi amor, mi amor para siempre,*' she cried as her passion reached a new high. '¡*Nunca me dejes!*'

In the morning, Mike once more took the wheel. He thought he saw the silver Renault again but could not be sure. He told himself he was being stupid, but the long-buried jungle survival instinct had stirred again.

In Morteaux, they found a bed-and-breakfast on the eastern edge of town. From their bedroom window, they looked up at the mountains of the Jura rising before them. Mike was pleased to note that the mountains were not as foreboding as he had expected. Signs told him that there were plentiful walking trails and forest grew high up on the slopes.

In the morning, after an early breakfast, they huddled over their maps and made their plans. Ruth said, 'It should only be a day's march to the hut. Our patrol could do it in less than a day, and we had to move carefully because of the Germans. We may have to bed down there overnight.'

## 238 Rue de Vincent, Paris, 1995

Left alone in the safe house, Giessner mulled over the entire business of the golden eagle. He was inclined to abort the entire operation. In Germany, he had assets and cash enough for two lifetimes; he needed no more. But the idea of owning the eagle kept elbowing its way into his mind. It had obsessed the Spaniards, so too Himmler and Borden and the French fireman. It was not possible to discount it's worth now. He decided to carry on, to call in some favours, long overdue.

He busied himself with the telephone books and a large, much-used notebook. Finally, he decided on his course of action. He placed his first call. Paul de Romnee was the son of a former Vichy official, arrested in Paris in 1943 by the Gestapo and charged with the murders of a string of prostitutes, all sexually mutilated and violently raped. He was sixteen years old. His father had paid the Gestapo agent a considerable sum of money to hush it all up. De Romnee, now retired, had served as a senior policeman for many years after the war. He would still have contacts.

The telephone answered right away, 'Who is this?'

The voice was that of an old man but carried a natural authority. 'You do not know me, but I know of you. Do you recall Paris in 1943? Do you remember Paulette, Suzanne, Dominique or Vivienne? I do.'

There was silence for a while, then, 'What do you want? You can prove nothing!'

'Ah, I see you do remember them, and no doubt a dozen more that were never found. I have a task for you. Failure will bring disclosure. Proof may be lacking, but the newspapers will love it. This is what you will do …'

The next morning the telephone rang. It was Otto. 'We are in Dijon,' he said, 'but we have discovered little. We found some old men in a bar who remember all the fuss about a stolen article in 1941. One, who was a railwayman at the time, said he heard the Germans had taken an entire train apart to find it, to no avail. There is an old rumour that the search moved near the Swiss border, to the mountains. For several weeks, a couple of Fieseler Storchs searched the area.'

'You are on the right track,' Giessner replied. 'Keep following. I may have some information for you by this afternoon. Call me at two o'clock.'

He waited by the telephone until noon. Shortly after, the telephone rang again. It was de Romnee. 'I have had my colleagues looking for your Land Rover. A certain Ms Ruth Grossmann hired it from Hertz in Paris three days ago. The rental is for one week. She did not give any details of where she intended to drive. I still have some influence here. I had a search conducted, and we saw the vehicle in the town of Morteaux this morning. The full license plate is 2154 BBY 147.'

'You have done well, my friend. Do not forget those lovely ladies from 1943. I may have need of your services again.'

## The Jura, France, 1995

Outside the bed-and-breakfast, they gathered at a café. 'Just one last decent cup of coffee before we go,' said Ruth. As they made their final plans, Mike noticed a small silver Renault parked across the street. Immediately, he felt his antennae picking up warning messages, but, as he watched the vehicle, a young woman wearing a blue anorak appeared, climbed in, and drove it away.

Their initial plan was straightforward. The Jura had undergone massive development since the last time Ruth had been here in 1945. The ski slopes and the walking trails now drew tourists from all over the world, so it was not possible for her to visualise the area as it had been in 1944. But it meant that they could drive much closer than they had expected. They had plotted a route from the road to the old survival hut. Now all they had to do was to follow the compass bearing to their destination. As they left the village, a small blue Mercedes Benz sedan pulled into the road behind them. They did not notice it.

Tourists crowded the area, many setting out on walking trails or just driving to take in the wonderful scenery. The going was not straightforward. They had to detour many times to get around crevasses and rock falls. By noon, they had made it to within a kilometre of their target. They brewed some coffee and ate. While they rested, Mike surveyed the slopes below them. There were several parties of walkers moving in their general direction, but nothing that looked suspicious. He bemoaned the fact that he had not remembered to add some field glasses to their shopping list.

## 238 Rue de Vincent, Paris, 1995

Giessner received the call from Otto just after dawn. They had found the Land Rover, and he was keeping a watch on it. He would call as soon as he knew where it went. The old Nazi smiled to himself. Now he was able to strike! He picked up the telephone and rang the airport, asking for his pilot.

Johannes Strasser had been on standby since the team had come to Paris and had expected instructions ever since. Now his instructions sent him to the flight office to hire a helicopter. Two hours later, he was airborne with his boss in the passenger seat, heading for the town of Morteaux.

## The Jura, near Morteaux, France, 1995

It took several hours to find their objective. The hut was easy to find, painted bright yellow and looking brand new. They checked the map reference again and redrew their course, but there was no doubt about it. This must be the place. But it wasn't. This hut was brand new and there was no sign that they had built it on the site of the old one.

Ruth sat on a rock and checked the maps meticulously. Mike looked down the slope again. There were two walking groups still approaching. They were getting closer, and he could make out some details. The first group comprised three men, all large and fit looking, wearing what appeared to be military style clothing. The second group looked like two men, or one man and a woman, the smaller one had a blue anorak and cap. What hair was visible was black.

Ruth called them over. 'Look,' she said, 'I have found the hut on the old topographic map. When I plotted its map reference, it is slightly different from the mountaineering map. It could be as much as two hundred meters up the slope from here.'

'Right,' said Mike. 'Spread out and move up there. There may be traces of the old hut left.' They moved slowly and searched the ground. Maria called out. 'Over here, I've found something.'

There were traces of charred timber on the ground and what looked like bits of rotted clothing and rusted food cans. It could only be the site of the old hut. Mike looked around 360 degrees. There was a small stream about fifty metres away and a few piles of jumbled boulders.

There was no trace of any hide or disturbed soil. The group of three men had drawn closer now, about one hundred metres away. There was no sign of the second group. Mike said, 'Let's wait for these people to pass by, so we might have an undisturbed time to look for it.'

They watched the three men approach. *'Bonjour,'* said Ruth, *'Comment allez-vous?'*

The men stopped, and, with no warning, two produced pistols. 'Better than you, you Jew bitch!' said the tall blonde man. 'Where is the golden eagle?'

Mike said, 'I don't know what you are talking about. We are just out for a walk. Why the guns?'

'You are going to find it for us. Start looking.' He motioned with his pistol. 'Do not try to run. We have a machine pistol. You will not get far.'

They began their search. For an hour or more, they searched in ever-widening circles. Finally, Maria stumbled and fell. Mike ran to her, anxious that she was injured. 'I have stumbled on something near this boulder,' she whispered, 'Look, there is something buried here.' They looked down to see a glint of something gold protruding from the ground, along with rotting pieces of oilskin. Mike quickly covered it up.

He was not quick enough. Otto ran to them. 'What is that?' he said, pushing them roughly aside. 'Let me look.' He knelt and uncovered the statue. He gave a gasp of appreciation as he held it up.

*'Mein Gott!'* This is more than any man could have imagined. We will all be rich!'

He stood and motioned for them to move to the side. 'Stay there,' he said. Mike could feel his hopes die away. He looked around and saw nothing but the Germans. Far away he could hear a helicopter growing louder as it approached. Soon it was hovering overhead, gingerly looking for a level place to land. Finally, it settled and cut its motor. The door opened, and an old man appeared in the opening. Ruth gave a gasp of fear. 'It is Giessner,' she cried. 'The monster.' Mike looked at the old man. He could tell by the computer-generated image that it was indeed Giessner.

Giessner looked at the two groups on the ground. He said to Otto, 'Have you found it?' 'Yes, we have, here it is.' He raised the statue high. Giessner reached for it, a greedy look on his face. He looked at Otto and smiled. 'Do it,' he said.

Mike knew what was coming. He took Maria's hand and squeezed it, looking with love into her eyes. *Not now,* he thought. *Now that I have found you at last.*

Otto drew back, and his other two men came forward. One opened his coat and produced a wicked-looking submachine gun. He ratcheted the cocking handle and looked at Otto for the signal to fire. Then his head came apart in a pink cloud. Otto and the other man froze in surprise. Before they could react. Ruth drew the Colt and fired. Both men collapsed into the snow. Ruth looked amazed. They turned to her; she was looking at the pistol in her hand. 'Impossible!' She said. Maria ran to her. 'Maria, I missed them. I know I did. I could not have hit both. I only fired one shot!'

Mike's instincts had cut in immediately. He ignored the women and pounced on the two men on the ground. But he needn't have bothered. Both were dead, shot in the back. 'It's okay,' he called to the two women. 'They are both dead. You didn't do it. They're shot in the back.'

Only now did he register the sound of the helicopter. At the first shot, it had restarted and blasted into the air; now it was receding into the distance. With it went the golden eagle. 'Well,' said Mike, 'That's that for the moment. It looks as though we will have to start all over again. What are we going to do with all this dead meat?'

Ruth said, 'We will look after that.'

Mike turned to her. 'We?' She gestured behind him. He swung around and saw a woman in a blue anorak approaching. Both she and her companion carried what looked like sniper rifles. No wonder the Germans had stood no chance. Mike looked at the man; he was swarthy, with jet-black hair and a large moustache. He looked like a Greek or an Iraqi.

'Ruth,' he said, 'what is going on here?'

She gave him a rueful smile. 'I am not French; well, not anymore. I am an Israeli, as are my two friends there. We are Mossad. When you came to me with your story, I saw a wonderful opportunity to get our hands on Giessner. We have been after him for fifty years. We saw in your search for the golden eagle a chance to bring him out into the open. Unfortunately, he has escaped justice once more. Please meet my friends. Yakov and Beth. Those are not their actual names, of course. We will continue our quest for the Nazi. If you care to join forces with us, we may have a better chance and you may recover the eagle. You can decide that later. Now, it is best that you return to Paris. We will clean up this mess. Come to my apartment at nine tomorrow evening. We will decide what to do after that.'

# THE SAFE HOUSE

### 238 Rue de Vincent, Paris, 1995

Giessner wasted no time once he returned to Paris. There, he went immediately to the house on *Rue de Vincent*, where he removed his personal possessions and issued instructions to his caretakers.

They were a husband and wife who maintained the house in his absence. They had been members of the SS and had been part of Giessner's retinue from the time he had been in Paraguay. The man had been a *SS-Sturmscharführer* (Senior Sergeant) of the concentration camps section. His wife had been a guard also, a member of the *SS-Helferin* with a vicious reputation for cruelty. They were old now, but still dangerous and always armed.

Within three hours, Giessner was airborne and heading for his fortified complex in the *Reichswald*, between the Dutch border and the German town of Kleve.

### Hotel Tour Eiffel, Paris, 1995

They had left Morteaux right away, leaving the bodies to the care of Ruth and her two colleagues. They had driven through the night and the next day, stopping for coffee, food and fuel, alternating drivers until they arrived in Paris in the early evening. Mike had telephoned the hotel and taken a room for two nights. He wanted a good bath, an excellent dinner and the arms of the beautiful woman by his side, for he needed comfort and time to decide what they should do.

She came to him, all lace and flashing eyes, her lips fusing with his, her arms around him. He took her to the bed, undressing her slowly, stroking and caressing her breasts, her stomach, her special places, until, joined as one, the fury of her orgasm drove him on to new highs. *'No Te detengas, no Te detengas, oh Dios, ¡Te quiero!'* she cried out in her passion. How magnificent she was. How could he be so lucky?

Lying in the afterglow, bodies entwined, he experienced a peace and fulfilment he had never known. 'Maria,' he whispered. 'I cannot be without you. What are we to do?'

She nestled her head into his shoulder. 'We must be together always.' she said. 'I will follow you wherever you go. I am yours and you are mine, nothing can ever change that.' In the morning, they breakfasted on their intimate little balcony. Both were starving. *'Cariño,'* she said, 'We must keep up our strength for each other.' She gave him that special smile again, and he felt his heart lurch. It would always do that to him.

Over breakfast, they discussed what they should do about the golden eagle. Mike was inclined to let it go. 'It will be difficult to find it now. We do not know Giessner's whereabouts or his current identity. When he wanted the eagle, it was easy to draw him out. Now that he has it, he does not need to come anywhere near us.'

'All that is true,' said Maria, 'but I want to continue. The eagle is of value to me because of my family's history, and I do not want an evil man to benefit from it. He should be caught and punished for his war crimes, at the very least. He has caused so much suffering.'

'Well,' said Mike. 'Perhaps Ruth and her Mossad companions will have something to say about that. Let's wait until tonight to see what they know. It might be easier than I think.'

## 1217 Rue des Soldats, Paris, 1995

Mike did not know it, but the Mossad has one of the most sophisticated and widespread intelligence networks in the world. Except for Asia, they have sympathetic people everywhere, namely just about every Jew in existence. While most of these would not betray their own countries, they welcomed with open arms any opportunity to assist in the roundup of Nazi criminals. This would continue until all Nazis were either captured or dead.

The Jews are a well-educated and intelligent people, well represented in the higher echelons of the public services and the professions. Many were 'sleepers' contactable by Mossad if required.

'Yakov' and his companions worked hard all afternoon, calling in favours and putting together a plan to find Giessner and bring him to justice. Ruth hoped that Mike and Maria would become involved. It would be an acceptable result for them if they could retrieve the golden eagle after investing so much in the search for it and the dangers they had faced. Besides, she probably had them to thank for her life.

By nine o'clock, the plans had gelled. Now they waited for Mike and Maria to arrive. Tonight, they would begin their quest.

Mike and Maria arrived exactly at nine. They sat at the kitchen table and drank coffee while Yakov briefed them. 'We have tracked down that telephone number *your* assailant, Ruth, was carrying, the one Mike called. It is an old house on 238 *Rue de Vincent*. We believe Giessner uses it as a safe house in Paris. The records show that there have been no calls made from the number; it must have been just for his men to report to him. There is another number that was used to make outside calls. There were several calls to Germany. We have the numbers; we might be able to trace them.'

Mike said, 'He will hardly be in Paris now that he has the eagle. He will have gone to ground in whatever hole he has been in for years, probably in Germany.'

'Quite so,' replied Yakov, 'But we have found out that there are two permanent residents, an old couple. My bet is that they are caretakers, probably old SS people, like Giessner. They would be the only ones he would trust.'

'Is there a record of who owns this house?' asked Maria.

'We have the name of a trust, set up in the Cayman Islands, and owned by a Swiss corporation whose directors are all officers of

*Die Miners Bank Aus Zurich.* This bank has links to many of the treasures the Nazis looted from all over occupied Europe. We can go no further there. The paper trail is a blind alley unless we can induce someone to talk.'

'What else do we know?' said Mike.

Beth answered this time. 'We have run surveillance on the house this evening while there was some light remaining. There were lights on inside the house, and I'm sure there are motion-activated lights outside. There are no dogs patrolling the grounds – they would activate the lights, but they may be there to be released if the lights come on.'

Mike raised an eyebrow. 'Access?'

Yakov said, 'We can get over the wall easily enough. Getting into the house might be a problem if we alert them. I think the best time to attempt it will be around three in the morning. I am sure they will be asleep by then.'

'What if they do have dogs? How are we to deal with them?' Maria said.

Yakov replied, 'We have silencers for our weapons. That will not be a problem, but we will have to use stealth with everything that we do. Mike, do you have any military experience?'

'I was an officer in the Australian army and spent a year sneaking around the jungle in Vietnam looking for the Viet Cong, if that's any use to you.'

'Excellent. You must be good at sneaking around because you survived. I think you will be useful after all. Now, this is what we are proposing…'

They discussed the plan in depth. Mike was used to planning operations, but he knew plans are apt to go to hell in a handbasket as soon as you fire the first shot, so he insisted on a simple plan. They agreed on a three-step plan.

The first step was to isolate the house by finding the master power switch and the telephone lines, as well as deal with any dogs that might be present. The second step was to get into the house as silently as possible, and the last step would be the interrogation of the occupants.

The three Mossad agents were all dressed in dark jeans and

roll-neck jerseys. They would wear balaclava face masks. Mike and Maria had come dressed in their military pants and boots. Ruth scurried into her bedroom and returned with a dark blue top for Maria. Mike's dark green shirt would do. They checked weapons. Ruth would leave her antiquated weapons behind. They would arm her and her companions with fearsome looking Mini-UZI machine pistols fitted with silencers. Mike understood now how they would deal with any dogs they found.

They offered Mike a Glock 17 pistol and a wicked-looking commando knife. He reckoned they would be adequate, but he hoped he would not have to use them. Ruth made coffee and they settled down to wait. Mike knew this was the worst part, waiting for an operation to begin. Nerves became frayed and tempers short before the adrenaline boost of action cut in. They retreated into their own little worlds and were silent.

Mike and Maria sat together, holding each other's hand, each drawing strength from the other. Maria worried; she had never taken part in anything like this before, but Mike seemed confident and that was good enough for her.

## *238 Rue de Vincent, Paris, 1995*

Herman Goss and his wife Irma had retired for the night. Before they did, Herman did his usual round of the building. He checked that all the windows were locked, and the door locks armed. The exterior lights were switched on and an electric lock could release the dogs by pressing a button beside his bed or in other parts of the house. He hesitated. All last week, those *verdammt* lights had been annoying him. All sorts of things had activated them, squirrels, rabbits and night birds. He had been getting up at all hours to release those *faulen hunde*. Herman was old, tired and querulous. He decided to turn off the lights and let the dogs out. They could handle any intruders.

Giessner had warned them that the group he had left in the Jura might try to get into the house in search of the golden eagle but he said they were amateurs. The dogs should look after them. He did not know that three of them were trained Mossad agents and a fourth had been a skilled soldier.

'I hope that Jew bitch tries,' said Herman. 'She will get what she deserves.' Despite the racial purity laws, he had no compunction in selecting any good-looking Jewish woman from the prisoners and brutally raping her. Irma laughed at him. 'Your wiener has long since shrivelled, old man. You wouldn't know what to do with her!'

He snarled and went off to bed. As he slumbered, a van drew up to the back of the house, tight alongside the wall. It was just before three in the morning. Silently, all five of them climbed to the roof of the vehicle. Yakov pushed an extension ladder over the wall to the ground below and made sure they securely bedded it to the wall and the ground.

Maria was to remain with the vehicle. Ruth was to lag behind the others and cover their backs. The other three separated and ran for the house as quickly and silently as they could. There was a lawn surrounding the house and the last fifty metres of their run was in plain view, no cover at all. Mike found himself stumbling over logs and bracken as he ran, having to lift his knees as high as he could before he reached the open lawn. He was surprised, as he had expected to be flooded with light. The security lights had failed to operate. *Good*, he thought, and headed for the house. The three of them would follow the walls, looking for the telephone junction box. One slash with his knife would do it.

He heard a kind of muffled snarl, followed by what sounded like someone tearing a sheet of calico apart. Mike had no time to even think about that when he heard a louder growl behind him and turned to see a black shape hurtling out of the darkness at him. He was lucky. He had drawn his knife in anticipation of cutting telephone wires; now that gave him just the split second he needed. He lifted his left forearm to shield his face and braced his feet with the knife held forward of him, slightly tilted up. The dog crashed into him, fangs clamping on his raised arm, but its weight carried it onto the knife. It knocked the blade from Mike's hand, but not before it had speared between two ribs and into the animal's heart.

Beth came running to him. 'Are you alright?' she whispered. Mike rolled the dog off him and sat up. 'That bloody hound needs to go to obedience school,' he said shakily. 'He just wouldn't stop!' He looked at his forearm. It was bleeding, but there was not much damage. He thanked the Gods that his tetanus shots were up to date, as he wrapped it in his handkerchief.

'Yakov met a dog too,' said Beth, 'but he had time to shoot it. I don't think there are any more.' She loped away into the darkness.

He headed to his right and carefully crept around the house, examining each opening as he went. His dull red torch showed him all the windows locked and, on some of them, he could see the wires of sensors. There was no way in there without setting off an alarm. He met the others at the back of the house, where they regrouped. Yakov said, 'We found the telephone wires and cut them, but the main switchboard must be inside the house. Do you think all the doors and windows are wired?'

Mike said that most of them he had seen were. 'There is a security system on the doors,' said Beth. 'We would have to be inside the house to disarm it.' Ruth had joined them. 'Can you do that?' she said. Yakov just smiled and nodded.

'Well,' she said. 'How are we to get in?'

Yakov said, 'Let's go around the house again for a closer look. Mike, you check where we have been. We will check your section.' Ruth stayed with him while the others disappeared into the gloom.

They moved slowly and kept their eyes on the base of the walls. They saw nothing until Ruth stumbled and fell headlong into the grass. Mike moved swiftly to the spot and scrabbled around with his hands. He felt what seemed like a right-angled wooden structure. He dug down further. The area was soft, not long covered with fresh soil. After a few minutes, he knew he had found a way in. 'Go get the others,' he said to Ruth. He drew his knife and kept on digging. Soon, he had exposed an old wooden door, probably an entrance to a cellar, long since disused.

All four were digging now. Soon the entire structure was exposed. It had a padlock and hasp, but the wood was so rotten with age that

Mike's knife made quick work of the latch. Yakov carefully examined the perimeter of the door and pronounced it free of wires. He lifted it on squeaky hinges and shone his torch inside.

There was a wooden ladder leading down into a basement. Carefully, they held on to Beth as she tried the ladder. She got down without difficulty, and as the second lightest, Ruth followed. Yakov caused the ladder to creak alarmingly, and the bottom rung broke away as he stepped on it. He stumbled to the floor. Mike eschewed the ladder and, with support from the others, slid down the side of the entrance. They were in a large basement, fitted with pipes and a heating furnace, an old-fashioned coal-fed machine with a firebox big enough to hold a small adult. It was long out of use. It seemed electricity now heated the house.

They found the main switch panel near a staircase leading up into the rest of the house. Yakov examined it carefully. 'I think I should disarm the alarm system first,' he said. 'It might have a failsafe circuit and cutting off the mains power may activate it. I won't be long.' He crept off slowly up the stairs.

He took about twenty minutes and came sliding back down the stairs. 'Just as well I went,' he said, 'we would have brought the house down.' He moved to the power board and flipped the master switch. There was no reaction.

'Right,' he said, 'let's go. They will be upstairs.'

Herman and Irma no longer shared a bed, not even a room. Long ago she had tired of his snoring and chronic flatulence and had moved to a small room at the end of the house as far away from the noise as possible. She always slept with a small night light on. Even now, she feared someone from her brutal past would come back for vengeance. She stirred and rolled over in the bed. Something was wrong! The light was out. She got out of bed and tried the switch; there was no mains power!

Yakov led them up the stairs to the second floor, towards the sound of loud snoring. Outside the door of the reverberating room, they paused before Yakov pushed it open and charged in, pointing his flashlight into the eyes of the bemused Herman, grabbed him and flung him back into the bed. Only then did he realise the man was alone.

Mike had not yet entered the room when he heard a scream of rage coming from the other end of the landing. He turned to see an apparition straight from a horror movie hurtling at him. There was a medley of wild hair, a flowing night dress, an open, screaming mouth and an upraised arm holding a long-bladed knife.

He had no time to react before she was upon him. Mike felt the knife sear along the top of his left shoulder as she knocked him to the floor with her weight; he saw the mad staring eyes and tried to grapple with her knife hand. She struck again at his torso. He tried to turn his body away from the blade but felt it slice down his side. Again, there was the sound of calico tearing and it flung the old woman from him to lie dead on the floor. She had taken almost half a magazine in her side from Ruth's UZI.

Dazed, he pulled himself into a sitting position. He was bleeding from his shoulder and his side, but he was not badly hurt. The old woman had sliced him up a little but he would be alright when he had stopped the bleeding. Ruth found a bathroom and came back with towels and a sheet she tore into bandages.

'Thanks,' he said. 'That was close.'

'Don't mention it,' she said. 'I already owed you one.'

In the bedroom, Herman was now fully awake. All his nightmares had come at once. He was facing two people with UZI submachine guns. Two more were outside on the landing. He saw the huddled body of his wife and he knew he would join her in Hell very soon.

'*Was ist das? Wer sind Sie?*' he croaked. Yakov replied in Yiddish, gratified to see his old eyes grow wide with terror. '*Juden!*' he cried. '*Nein, nein!*'

Yakov switched back to German. He had made his point. 'Now, you Nazi bastard, you will tell us where Giessner has gone and where we will find him. We already know he is in Germany, but your information will save us a lot of time.'

'I will tell you nothing, Jew.'

'Well, we will have to persuade you to do so. I am sure you are familiar with all the methods of torture. After all, you have had a lot of practice, haven't you?'

The old man looked at him with defiance. '*Ja*, I have been responsible for removing many thousands of you vermin from the world.' He looked at Mike. 'You do not look like a Jew. What are you?'

'Unlike you, I am a human being,' said Mike. 'I am proud that my father fought against you and your madness. You are nothing but cowardly scum.' He turned to Yakov. 'I have an idea,' he said. 'I don't think any threats of conventional pain will work with him, but I think I know what to do.'

'How will you do that?'

'I think we should give to him what he gave to his victims,' said Mike. 'Come with me, the ladies will keep him under control.'

Half an hour later, Yakov returned. He looked at Herman. 'Come,' he said. 'We do not have any cattle wagons, but we will get you there, anyway.'

'Where? Where are you going to take me?'

Yakov seized him and frogmarched him out the door. 'Like your victims,' he said, 'you are going to the ovens!' They dragged him down to the basement. There, just beginning to glow, was the fire that Mike had lit in the old furnace.

'We are going to feed you into that oven feet first,' said Yakov. 'Now you will know how the Jews felt. We will have to wait a little while until the fire is ready. In the meantime, you should consider giving us the information we require. We will not harm you if you do. Now, where is Giessner, where is his house, how many men does he have with him and what are his security arrangements?'

Herman looked at him. There was terror in his eyes. 'You cannot do this to me. There are laws. I was only obeying orders. *Der Führer* issued them himself. He had to rid the world of *der Juden und der Bolsheviks!* It had to be done to save *das Vaterland*.'

Yakov did not answer him. Instead, he moved to the fire and inspected the coals, now building into a dull red mass below the flames. He turned to the women. 'I think it is almost ready.'

Ruth produced an enormous pair of scissors she had found in the bathroom. 'Now,' she said, 'we will obey the orders of the camp commandant. First, we remove your hair, and you will strip while Yakov here will conduct an internal examination to ensure you are not concealing valuables. After that, we will remove any teeth you have with gold fillings. Mike there has a large pair of pliers. Then you will go to the oven. After all, we are only removing vermin from the world, an activity you found so necessary.'

Herman began a high-pitched keening. His body shook, and his bladder and his bowels voided themselves in his terror. The smell was horrible. He began crying, '*Nein, nein, Gott hilf mir, hilf mir!*'

'You do well to speak of God,' said Beth. 'Soon you will be in His presence. He will have a special place ready for you.'

Ruth hacked away at his sparse hair. When she had finished, Yakov said to him, 'Now, off with your clothes. I have an inspection to carry out.' He picked up a screwdriver from the workbench.

That was all it took. Herman fell to his knees and pleaded to tell them all he knew. He babbled information as fast as he could until he was empty. He told them of maps concealed in the house's roof and how to get them. Finally, he collapsed.

'You weren't really going to put him in the furnace, were you?'

'Perhaps,' said Yakov. 'But now we don't have to, do we?' He turned and fired a short burst into the prone figure.

'You said you wouldn't harm him,' said Mike.

'Yes,' said Yakov, 'I lied.'

Maria met them halfway to the wall. She rushed to Mike, horrified by his wounds, frightened that he was gravely hurt. 'I'm okay,' he said. 'Tonight, you can wash and dress my wounds; it should be fun.'

The firefighters of *Caserne de Pompiers 28* rushed to a burning house in the *Rue de Vincent*. By the time they got there, the building was well-enveloped. They had hardly rolled out their hoses when the explosions began; Giessner had stored ammunition and explosives in the building. The captain quickly decided that his men's lives were at stake and ordered them away. They watched as the building burned to the ground.

# DAS VATERLAND

*Kleve, Germany, 1995*

Mike and Maria left Paris early in the morning. They took a train north and east, through Belgium to Köln. Here the train turned north again to the city of Düsseldorf. They changed trains and travelled north and west to the small city of Kleve. Kleve is situated near the *Reichswald*, a large thick forest of conifers, favoured by hunters in season and hikers in the brief summer. It runs almost to the Dutch border. There are many remote and wild areas and in the most remote of them Giessner had built his home.

It was a large house, built into a slope so that the ground floor had nothing but earth behind it. Into the hill he had built storage rooms and a confinement cell. He had stored weapons, ammunition and explosives. The cell was used as a punishment area for any of his men who needed to be disciplined. Not that there were many left; he had lost eight already. There were only five, including himself and his aide, Siegfried, who would not be much good in the rough stuff. But he did not worry. His motion sensors and dogs and security locks would protect him until he could recruit more from the ranks of the neo-Nazis.

He bemoaned the quality of such men. They were dim-witted and hard to teach. Once he had them, he could impart the hard lessons of the SS training he had as a youth, but still, they would never compare with those magnificent young men of 1940-44 who had come so close to total victory. Still, he had to work with what he had and make the most of it.

He had built the house with Polish labour, confined to the site while they did it, and taken back to their homes in Poland. No locals had knowledge of what was in the building or of its security measures. He had carefully kept most of the trees so that aerial views were partly obscured. Most people thought it was a rich man's hunting lodge.

Access by road was made more difficult by driving a tunnel into the side of the hill a hundred metres away from the house and using a logging track to get to its camouflaged entrance, the vehicles invisible to the casual observer.

Now he sat in his library, cut deep into the hillside, where the place of honour went to a leather-bound and autographed copy of *'Mein Kampf'*. There were pictures of himself and other notables in their sinister black and silver uniforms, and a swastika flag hung on the wall alongside a framed picture of *Der Führer*. Here, he could relive the glory days of his youth. Only his secretary knew of the existence of this room. It had a separate security system and he was the only one who could access it. He had no wife; he had never married. When the fancy took him, he would fly to Berlin or Paris, where there were girls who would do anything for the right price.

Now he had the *Steinadler*, nothing else mattered. He had it on his desk, where he could admire it all day. At night it lived in a safe. He was a little puzzled, however. Sometimes he could almost believe that the majestic bird looked at him with amused contempt. When he placed it in the safe once, he imagined it had looked at him in a malevolent manner. He thought it was probably a change in the light. He had not considered selling it, but he would like to have a current valuation. Ten million American dollars would not surprise him.

## Hotel Bismarck, Kleve, Germany, 1995

The five of them huddled around a table in Mike and Maria's room, planning their attack on Giessner's fortress. It was becoming increasingly obvious that it might be an impossible task. The Mossad agents had travelled by Land Rover from Paris. There were no border checks anymore, so they could bring all the weapons and equipment they needed. But when they met over the maps and plans, Mike said, 'I think we might need my old company and a troop of tanks to get in there. It looks impossible.'

Yakov said, 'Yes, it will be difficult, but we know he is down to four men now. He will have trouble covering the whole place. If we caused a diversion, we may be able to distract his men and deal with them one at a time. He will depend heavily on his warning systems now.'

They talked it over and over. Finally, Yakov decided they would do a reconnaissance early in the morning. He would do this himself along with Beth. The others could drop them off on the road nearest the rear of the house and do their own patrol in the vehicle before coming back to pick them up.

They set off just before daylight. Mike was pleased to see that the Land Rover was a dark green colour; it would blend in nicely with the forest. They eventually came down a rough forester's track and halted. The house was about a kilometre away. Yakov and Beth dressed as hikers in casual clothes and heavy boots. They left their UZIs behind, carrying just their pistols. After about fifty metres, the forest closed around them, and they vanished from sight. Mike eased the Land Rover into gear and moved off.

Their vehicle reconnaissance revealed little. They found the concealed entrance to the vehicular tunnel and spotted some of the security lights, but they could not see much of the house from the forest track. They hoped the others were having better luck.

The pair had eased their way into the forest. There was only light undergrowth and some bracken fern; the mature trees had stood for a hundred years at least and had shaded out all but the most determined low-growing plants. They spied several game trails through the brush. Beth knew that there were plenty of deer and wild pigs around, so they progressed slowly, not wanting to spook them. As they got closer to the house, they walked as soundlessly as possible.

From the embankment, they could see the windows on the top level of the house. There was a small, paved area here with some outdoor furniture accessible from the house via a large, solid door. Back up the slope, there were two large tubes protruding from the ground, topped with weather shields. Beth said, 'What do you think they are?'

'They have no scorch marks, so they aren't smokestacks; it wouldn't surprise me if they are ventilation tubes. Remember, there are underground rooms below there.' They could not get any closer; it would look suspicious, so they withdrew a little and moved around the house to the west.

Suddenly, there was a crash in the undergrowth and a small group of deer hurtled past them. Yakov pulled Beth into the cover of the bracken and put his finger to his lips. 'They're disturbed,' he whispered. 'Listen.'

For a few minutes, there were only the diminishing sounds of the fast-disappearing animals, but soon they could hear faint whistling. It was a popular song; whoever was responsible for it was nice and relaxed. Yakov and Beth crept forward towards the sound. They found a rough-looking young man leaning over a small deer, skinning it. Beside him was a bow and a quiver of arrows. 'So that is why we heard nothing,' whispered Beth. 'Do you think he is from the house?'

'He looks like one of their tough guys,' said Yakov. 'Should we take him out?' She hesitated and said, 'We might lose the element of surprise if they have a missing man. Perhaps we should leave him alone.'

Seconds later, the decision was taken out of their hands. A dog barked. The man straightened up and looked about. They had not noticed the animal lying in the shade behind the hunter. Now the man moved towards them. They saw that the man tied the dog to a tree and relaxed a little. '*Wer ist da?*' called the young man.

They looked at each other. Yakov nodded. 'The sucker punch,' was all he said. Beth moved out of cover and sauntered towards the man. She had undone the top three buttons of her blouse, and she smiled invitingly at him. 'Hello,' she said. 'Who are you? I was just taking a walk in the woods.' She gave a throaty laugh. 'I never imagined I would meet a hunk like you.' He smiled a broad smile, almost a leer.

'What are you doing alone, sweetie?' he said. 'There could be evil men out here. They might take advantage of someone like you.'

She simpered and struck a seductive pose. She giggled. 'That's just what I was hoping for. What is your name?' He ogled her low neckline. Two-thirds of her breasts were clearly visible. She moved to him and put her arms around his waist.

Gregor Lipski had been at the house near to six months now, as frustrated as any red-blooded man could be. He saw those red lips and luscious breasts and all sense left him. *Mein Gott, this is going to be good!* He clumsily reached for her, but she skipped away. 'Come over here,' she said. 'I have my sleeping bag. It will be much more comfortable.'

As he followed her into the undergrowth, an iron-hard arm took him around the throat. He felt the muzzle of a pistol grinding into the base of his spine, and he heard a harsh voice. 'Be still, or I will blow away your backbone!'

He looked in fury at the girl. 'Oh dear,' she said, 'I forgot to tell you my husband was here. He is a very jealous type. You would not be the first of my lovers he has killed or crippled.' Gregor had fallen for the oldest trick in the book.

They took him further into the forest, away from the house, and near to the road. There they waited until they heard the Land Rover stop slowly. At the vehicle, Yakov smiled at Mike. 'Look what we found,' he said. 'I think he might be up for a brief chat.' Mike stepped down from the vehicle. He decided to repeat his little trick with Kurt that had worked so well among the Elm trees of Oxford.

'Tell me your name, boy,' he said. 'I am sure we will have a lot to talk about. We are not really interested in you, just your Nazi boss. Surely you don't wish to perish for an old war criminal who just uses you and pays you a pittance, do you?'

'*Ich bin Gregor,*' he said, '*Ich werde Ihnen sagen, nichts!*'

Mike smiled at him. 'You are a long way from your friends now. I'd bet that it would take a long time to find you out here. Anyway, I was about to ask you if you liked the girls, but I guess you have already shown us that.'

'*Ich spreche kein Englisch!*' he cried. Mike shook his head. 'I think you know enough,' he said, 'But you won't need much to understand me.' The others threw him to the ground and bound him up with duct tape.

Mike reached down and cut away the clothes at his groin, revealing his genitals. Dramatically, he ran his fingers along the edge of the knife. 'Well, what is it to be? Will you speak now, or will I remove a few bits first?'

Gregor tried to struggle, but they had bound him tightly. 'He looked around with wide staring eyes. '*Nein, nein*, you cannot do it.' Mike squatted alongside him. 'In Australia, you know, back on the farm, I castrated thousands of lambs. They all survived, but none of them turned into rams. I guess they just weren't interested.' He leaned over and gently pricked the man's scrotum with the point of the knife; a little trickle of blood ran down onto his leg. Gregor screamed and tried to scrabble away, but he was held too tightly. Mike said, 'Left one or right one, or perhaps a couple of centimetres off here?' He touched the blade to his penis.

Gregor began to blubber. 'What do you want to know?' he sobbed.

The Mossad wanted to kill him, arguing that he would only go back and report them. Maria said, 'He will not do that. If he does, surely Giessner will do the job for us. Besides, the wallet he carries reveals the location of his family. It is a long way away, but we could come for him there.' They took him back to town and purchased him a one-way ticket to his home in Vienna; they took all his documents and money and made sure he boarded, watching as the train left the station. Back at the hotel, they sat down to review the additional information he had given them.

## The Reischwald, Germany, 1995

Giessner sat stony-faced and listened to the report about the missing Gregor. When he had not returned from his brief hunting trip, the others had gone to find him. They found the dog and the carcass of the deer along with his bow and arrows, but there was no sign of him.

After thinking about it for a while, one other said, 'Well, he was a hell of a lover, according to him. I know he had a girl in *Kleve* and recently he has been complaining about how randy he was. Could he have gone to her?' That incensed Giessner. All his men had strict instructions to avoid Kleve like the plague. He did not want any information about the house to leak out. His men were told to cross the border to Holland if they had to go somewhere. Now they would go nowhere. There were not enough of them.

While the others watched, he entered one of his rages, red-faced, eyes bulging, right arm raised. He screamed, cursed and threatened for over ten minutes. They knew better than to disturb him until the rage had passed. When it did, Giessner turned to Siegfried and issued an order. 'Telephone Johannes Strasser and get him to check on the girlfriend. Then he is to come here. We will need another man now that bastard Gregor has run away.'

*What is happening?* he wondered. *Could the Spanish woman and her friends be this close?* He had discounted them, for he knew they were only amateurs, adventurers looking for the eagle. He had not stayed around long enough in the Jura to see the ones who had killed Otto and the others. They may even have been police.

Siegfried returned. 'Johannes is on his way,' he said, 'but a friend in Paris faxed this to me.' He handed Giessner a document. Giessner read it and his face lost its colour. He looked up. 'This is a newspaper report from Paris. Someone has burnt our safe house on *Rue de Vincent* down. They recovered two bodies, both too severely burnt to identify, both shot at close range.'

'Maybe old Herman finally cracked and blew away that old *hündin* of his. God knows he should have done it a long time ago,' quipped another of the men.

Giessner was not amused. 'It is too much of a coincidence,' he said. 'That woman must have been involved.'

'Herman would never tell them anything. He's too tough for that.'

'Herman was an old man. Who knows what he did?'

## Hotel Bismarck, Kleve, Germany, 1995

Gregor had told them not a lot more than they knew, but he confirmed that the pipes at the rear of the house were ventilators that drew fresh air into the lower rooms. They were large pipes equipped with interior ladders to facilitate maintenance. Now they had a way in but did not know if Giessner would have them monitored. However, he was low on men, and they all agreed a diversion would be the way to draw some of them away.

There are two factors that bedevil anyone trying to prevent access to a building. Every building needs sewerage and drainage. While the sewerage system was too small, Gregor had confirmed that the central courtyard had a large drain that took stormwater away down the slope of the hill near the vehicle tunnel, thence into the road's drainage ditches. He calculated it was large enough to accommodate a man. He remarked he did not understand why it was so big.

They pored over the maps and layouts. Finally, they came up with a plan. Mike would take one of the UZIs and attempt to approach the front of the building. His aim was to eliminate any dogs and to draw away anyone who came to investigate.

This time, Maria refused to let him go without her. No amount of pleading could convince her to remain out of harm's way. The others would attempt to climb down the ventilation pipes. Mike said, 'It would be good for you to have some stun grenades to drop down first, just in case someone is waiting.'

Yakov said, 'I'll try to improvise. There is a store here that sells fireworks; maybe they have something suitable.' He set off to do his shopping.

## The Reischwald, Germany, 1995

At three o'clock, the sky was dark and there was only a slight crescent moon providing concealment but not making it too difficult to see. Mike and Maria moved quietly towards the wall at the front of the house. It was a rough stone wall and they were confident they would find enough foot and hand holds to scale it.

Up they went and sat on top of the wall. All was quiet. Mike gave her a last kiss and dropped to the ground below. He caught her as she came down. 'Stay behind me and watch my back now, quiet as a mouse.'

They headed into the grounds. Like the house in Paris, there was an empty space nearer the building. Now their job was to attract attention. Soon they crossed a beam from a sensor.

A forest of lights lit up the front of the house and an alarm bell began to ring; they dashed back into the darkness behind the beams.

Then they heard the barking. It came from the left, along the side of the house. Two Dobermans rushed into the glare, hesitated and headed right towards them. They terrified Maria. Mike pulled her further into the gloom. 'Stay close behind me,' he said. 'Give them only one target.'

The dogs hurtled onwards. They were about four metres away when Mike squeezed his trigger. Once more there was the ripping of calico and both dogs went down in a tangled heap. One writhed a little and gave a howl before expiring.

'Oh, the poor things,' said Maria, 'they were only doing their jobs.'

Mike said, 'Just like the Nazis in 1943. Stay still and quiet. Their handlers might come looking for them.'

The lights went off. There was no movement to trip the sensors. Still, they waited. Then Mike saw movement near the house; a man in a black coat was approaching slowly, calling out quietly, 'Boris, Boris.' The lights came on again.

Boris was beyond responding, but Mike let out a sound like a dog whining in pain. The man started running towards them into the dark behind the lights only to be met by Mike, who stepped into his path and smashed his left elbow across the bridge of his nose. He went down as though shot. Quickly, Mike cuffed his ankles and wrists with plastic zip ties.

Only a sharp knife could release him now. The man was unconscious. They made sure his airways were clear and laid him in the recovery position, stuffed his handkerchief into his mouth and gagged him.

Yakov had been busy with his fireworks before they set out. He had purchased several big thunderclaps, about ten inches long and an inch in diameter. With some duct tape, he made bundles of four and twisted the fuses together. He hoped the flash and concussion of the four exploding together would work a little like a stun grenade. Now was the time to find out. He lit two and gave one to Beth. Ruth was to wait outside and cover their backs. They each dropped their 'bombs' down the ventilator shafts.

The noise was astounding. Before the reverberations had died away, they were scurrying down the ladders. At the bottom, Yakov found nothing, just the stink of gunpowder. Beth had more luck. She came down in a rush to crouch on the floor. Before her, she saw Johannes, the pilot, flat on his back and unconscious, nose, eyes and ears bleeding. She restrained him with zip ties and used another to affix his wrists to the bottom rung of the ladder. He was going nowhere in a hurry.

She looked around the room. There was an open space outfitted like a gym and a door leading out towards the front of the house. She looked up the shaft and called Ruth to come down. When she was down, they approached the door.

Ruth carefully opened it. They were in a wide corridor. Alongside them, a similar door stood open, Yakov leaning against the opening. 'Welcome to the dungeons,' he said.

Inside the second space was a large cell. 'Looks pretty good,' he said. 'Where to from here?'

They crept down the corridor, carefully opening each door in commando fashion. They found nobody. At the end of the corridor, there was a large room, festooned with all the paraphernalia of a hunting lodge – shields, banners, mounted heads of unfortunate animals and a large banqueting table. Stairs led off on both sides to a mezzanine floor overlooking the hall. There was no one in view.

This puzzled Yakov. There should have been more reaction to their entry. He did a quick count. They had one of Giessner's men. There should have been three, so there were only two remaining. But where were they? Suddenly, the large room flooded with light.

At first, they feared someone had discovered them, then realised that the outside lights had come on. Beth ran to a window and called the other two over. Out on the front lawn, a man was creeping, calling out, looking for someone without result. Yakov wanted to shoot him on the spot, but he did not want to leave any dead bodies lying around in the open if he could avoid it.

'Ruth,' he said, 'Keep an eye on that fellow. Shoot him if you must, but don't let him out of your sight. We will go after the others.'

In his library, locked away with his treasures, the former *Obersturmbannführer* Rolo Giessner, pride of the *SS*, scourge of the Jews, hero of the third Reich, sat terrified. He had heard the thunderclaps detonate and was sure that troops were swarming through his house, ready to take him away for his ultimate punishment.

He looked at the eagle with rheumy eyes. In the last few days, he imagined he had seen its eyes move and the expression in them change. Each time he looked, it appeared to be more malevolent, almost evil. Now he turned it away and admired it from behind.

The night he had returned from Paris, the dream had begun. It filled his night with the screams of the wounded and the victims. He saw the trenches open and all the Jews he had ordered to be shot begin to clamber out, reaching for him with their rotting hands. He heard the cries of the burning British soldiers and, above all, the scream of an eagle; he saw its eyes, glittering, evil, filled with hate, and he woke screaming himself, covered in perspiration.

By the morning, he had rationalised away his nightmare. In the cold light of day, it seemed a little childish, but that night it came again, more horrible, demonic and full of the flames of hell. He saw the gleaming eyes again and a burning swastika flag amidst the rubble of a bombed-out city. He knew he was dreaming, but he could not force himself awake, no matter how he struggled; the dead Jews came for him again and pulled him screaming down into the trench with them. The earth poured back into the trench, burying him. He woke trembling with fear. Last night he had not slept at all for fear of the dream.

This morning, Siegfried had noticed the change in him, his bleary and bloodshot eyes, his ashen face and his trembling body. He could not raise a cup of coffee without spilling it, so badly did his hands shake. Siegfried said nothing. He did not want to risk his master's wrath.

The wrath had come, though, in the forenoon when Gregor had gone missing. After that meeting, he had collapsed and eventually, he had come to this room. Now, as he heard the explosions outside, he dared not come out.

Outside, Mike and Maria had moved away to the vehicular tunnel, keeping out of the floodlit area, looking for the stormwater drain. After half an hour, they found it. Gregor had been right; it was just about large enough for a man. A big man would have to crouch or use his hands and knees.

Maria shone her torch around the opening and into the drain. She gave an exclamation of surprise. 'Mike, can you see that shiny thing in there?' Together, they moved into the drain. What Maria had seen was, in fact, a motorcycle. Mike wheeled it out into the open. It was full of fuel and ready to go, with two large panniers on the back. He opened one of them.

Inside he found tightly packed bundles of high denomination notes, Sterling, US Dollars, Deutschemarks and Swiss Francs. There was a leather wallet containing US, Swiss and Dutch passports, all of which contained recent photos of Giessner. He knew what this was; it was Giessner's escape route. From here he could be in Holland in an hour or so.

He explained all this to Maria. 'We should put a stop to this,' she said, 'let's immobilise the bike.' They took all the documents and money from the pannier and concealed them in a shallow hole covered with rocks and brush. Mike wheeled it away a few metres and emptied the fuel tank before he put it back in the drain.

Ruth had watched the man on the lawn walking slowly back and forth, calling out something softly. Abruptly, he stopped. The movement sensors switched off the lights. *'Merde,'* she muttered and moved swiftly to the doors. They were locked, and she did not know the key sequence to open them.

Ruth hammered on the doors, hoping to attract him; perhaps he would open the door, but he did not. She had lost him! She looked frantically about, but the only way out was back the way she had come. Ruth ran back down the corridor, looking for the others. They were not in evidence, so she turned and ran back and up to the mezzanine level. Another corridor ran back from this level and she cautiously moved along it, checking every door as she went.

Yakov and Beth had been along the same corridor and found

nothing, but they had noticed that there was a length of wall, big enough for two rooms, without a door. At the end of the corridor, there was a spiral staircase up to a third level. He gestured to it and said, 'There must be three levels. The plans said nothing about this.'

'There may have been modifications made after they lodged the plans,' said Beth, 'a special or secret room perhaps, or an escape route to the roof or a viewing deck.'

They climbed the stairs to find a small landing with a door. The door was shut and there was no visible handle or lock of any kind. They turned back down the stairs. When they reached the bottom, they found Ruth there, waiting for them. 'Yakov,' she said, 'I lost our man on the front lawn. He moved out of sight just as the lights went out. I tried to get out the front door to follow him, but the doors were locked. I do not know where he has gone.'

A voice behind them said, 'Wonder no more. He is right here. Be very careful, for I have a gun.'

They swung around. Siegfried stood rigid, a machine pistol in his hands. He looked tense and scared, and the muzzle of the gun wavered back and forth. Yakov worried. A scared man with a gun was more dangerous than a professional. He might shoot at any moment, and this man was far from a professional gunman. He was an effeminate-looking, pasty-complexioned man. Yakov guessed he spent most of his time in an office.

'Okay,' he said. 'Keep calm. We will put our weapons on the floor. Move carefully, ladies.'

Siegfried looked a little relieved at that, but Yakov decided to give him something more to worry about. 'We've beaten you, you know. You're the last man standing. Soon the police will be here. Don't make it harder on yourself. Murder will see you put away for life, and there are some big scary men in jail who would appreciate a little playtime with you. You had best put down your weapon. We will speak up for you, you know. Giessner cannot hurt you, he is neutralised now.'

The man looked more confused now, but he feared Giessner more than the police, it seemed. He gestured to them to move back down the corridor to the door before the blank wall they had been curious about. 'Inside,' he ordered. They entered a room that looked like a sitting room in a gentlemen's club, all dark wood panelling and leather easy chairs. He made them sit together on a sofa before he went to a desk and, reaching under it to a hidden compartment, withdrew a telephone handpiece. He picked it up and pushed a button on its base.

They could hear the querulous voice of an old man. '*Ja, was ist das?*'

'*Es ist Siegfried*, I have captured the invaders. There are three of them, a man and two women. They all look like *Juden*.'

They could hear the relief in the old man's voice. 'Bring them up,' he said. 'It's fifty years too late, but we can still exterminate them!'

Siegfried motioned them to the door. 'We will climb the staircase now. Remember, I am right behind you.' Yakov racked his brains for a way to reach the gunman. But it was impossible. He remained far enough away to shoot if they tried anything. Yakov had been ready to fake a fall from the staircase back onto him, but he was just too far back for that to work.

The door at the top of the stairs was open. Siegfried prodded them all through the door. Giessner was waiting to meet them, pistol in hand. He made them sit together on the floor. They looked around at the display of Nazi artefacts. It was monstrous, unbelievable, that someone could worship such things now. They all felt revulsion at the sight.

Giessner stood before them. He looked confident now, in charge again. 'Well,' he said, 'Just like all the others, it has fallen to me to eliminate you. It will be an immense pleasure knowing I am carrying on *Der Führer's* work. We should have done it fifty years ago, but our people were weak. They could not stomach what we had to do. Siegfried, watch them. It is time for me to go. I must take *der Reichsführer's* eagle with me. I will go to America and sell it. It is worth millions; it will enable me to carry on *Der Führer's* work once more.'

Yakov said, 'Your kind always run and hide. You ran from the Russians, from the British and Americans, from justice. You are bullies and cowards. You will not prosper.'

A mad look crept into Giessner's eyes; he paced back and forth, speaking in German. What he said was like all the Nazi ravings anyone who had seen Hitler make a speech knew extremely well. As he raved, he held his arm up in a Nazi salute; he went red in the face and spittle dripped down his chin. Yakov hoped he would have a stroke or a seizure or something equally fatal, but he gradually calmed down. He picked up a small case and placed it along a section of the bookcase. He pressed somewhere on a shelf and a section of the bookcase swung open. There was a small landing behind it, with a ladder leading down.

'So,' he said, 'we did not prosper? We removed over five million *Jüdischen Ratten* from the world. You will go to join them. Tell them there are plenty of us still killing them! Tell them we will prevail. *Heil Hitler!*' His rage grew once more, and he began to scream invective at the *Juden*.

Mike and Maria had seen Siegfried cross the lawn. 'Come on,' whispered Mike, 'come on, come on, come closer.' But the man had veered around to the left of the building and disappeared into the shadows. The lights went off. They waited, but no sound came from the house. After a while, Mike said, 'I'm a bit worried about this. Nothing appears to be happening. Do you think we should have a look up this drain? If this is his escape route, it should take us right into the house.'

Maria said, 'It can't hurt. I can always say I picked you up from a gutter!' She smiled that smile again. He went to her and gently kissed her lips.

'Keep behind me and keep that pistol handy.' He switched on his torch and moved into the tunnel.

It was only just high enough; from time to time, they had to duck their heads and at one point the shaft narrowed alarmingly, but they made their way steadily along it. About fifty metres in, a smaller shaft joined theirs. 'I reckon that's where the drainage from the vehicular tunnel comes in,' said Maria. They went on.

The shaft continued almost straight ahead. The floor was damp and sloped upward gently as they proceeded. Suddenly, Mike stopped and turned off his torch. Maria breathed into his ear. 'What's wrong?'

He whispered back, 'I can see a faint light up ahead, go very carefully now, and try to be ultra-quiet; we must be getting close.' In another twenty metres, they came to a vertical shaft down which the faint light shone. There was a steel ladder welded inside the shaft. Away to their right, the drain continued. 'I bet that goes up to the central courtyard Gregor told us about,' said Maria.

Mike held his finger to his lips. There was a faraway murmur of voices, and the noise increased tenfold. 'It sounds as though someone is making an angry speech,' he said. 'I think I'll go up to see what is going on. You wait here. Be vigilant. That other man may still be outside and may have followed us up the tunnel.'

Giessner's tirade was slowing; the colour drained from his face and his eyes took on a more normal look. He went to a desk and picked up the golden eagle. It was heavy, and he struggled to lift it into a backpack that he strapped to his back. When he had steadied himself on his feet, he said to Siegfried, 'Give me the machine pistol. I want to kill these vermin myself.'

Siegfried took the weapon to him. 'Siegfried,' he said, 'you have been an excellent secretary to me for a long time now. You cannot come with me where I am going, and, sadly, I can leave no witnesses for our friends the *Polizei.*' He turned to his man and fired a short burst into his chest before he swung back to his three prisoners. 'Welcome to Hell,' he said and raised the weapon.

Yakov was about to make a last desperate bid to stop him. He figured he might be able to leap on him; he would die, of course, but he might save the women. But, as he tensed his body to try, a loud voice rang out.

'Drop the gun, you bastard! You're a dead man.'

The startled Giessner turned his head and Yakov took his chance. He propelled himself off the floor and hurtled into Giessner's chest. The weight of the eagle on his back took him to the floor. He fired, a wild burst that scythed across the room, shattering the photographs and knocking over his prized book, peppering the walls with bullet holes; the magazine emptied and the machine pistol clicked to a stop. Mike had crossed the room in an instant and helped Yakov to restrain his prisoner.

Both men were about to deliver him a good beating when Ruth cried, 'Stop, stop, don't damage him. We need him to stand trial in Israel. We need to show the world these animals will never be safe!'

The blood lust ebbed away from Yakov's brain. Slowly, he got to his feet. Already Beth was at work with her zip ties. Giessner was theirs.

Mike took the eagle from the pack and thrust it into his face. 'Look for the last time, you prick. You will never see this again.'

Giessner looked at the bird. The eyes were changing! They looked at him with an evil satisfaction. *'Nein, nein,'* he cried, *'der Steinadler ist verflucht.* Take it away!'

# WRAPPING UP

### Den Haag, Nederland, 1995

It had been an interesting trip from the *Reischwald*. They had placed Giessner in the back of the Land Rover and ditched all the weapons and equipment. The passports and the currency notes were all they had kept.

They crossed into Holland before sunrise near the small town of Plak without incident and began a non-stop drive for Den Haag, or, in English, The Hague, where the Israeli embassy is situated. They had telephoned ahead to Yakov's counterpart and a professional snatch squad of the Mossad, trained especially for this kind of extraction, took over their prisoner about halfway to their destination.

They gave him to the squad but kept the eagle and the banknotes. Yakov said to Maria, 'You have put in a great deal of work on this one. Without your help, we would never have found and captured him. Keep this money. You are going to relinquish your eagle I know, for its value to history and archaeology; it is worth many millions. You must have some reward for putting your lives on the line.'

She looked at Mike, who shrugged his shoulders, reluctantly accepting the money.

The extraction team kept Giessner partly tranquilised and sleeping until they got him to the embassy. The next morning, a Boing 747 of El Al Airlines took off in the pre-dawn darkness. Those aboard included an old man travelling on a Swiss passport, who slept most of the way. Before dusk, he awoke in a heavily guarded cell in a secret location in Tel Aviv.

That same afternoon, Mike and Maria took the statue to the Spanish embassy and asked for a meeting with the Ambassador and the Chief Cultural Attaché. The receptionist gave them the standard answer. The two officials were in a meeting and could not be disturbed. They were to come back in the morning; perhaps they would see them then.

Maria did an impression of a real volcano, a large one, erupting. With flashing eyes and waving hands, she let loose a stream of Spanish that was long and fiery. It was too fast for Mike to understand it, but it resulted in two officials fawning over her and trying to calm her down. Twenty minutes later, they were in the Ambassador's office.

The Ambassador was a patrician-looking man with an aristocratic name and an appreciation of Maria, who had shamelessly used *her* full name. The Cultural Attaché was a fashionably dressed woman in her early forties. Maria recognised her name; she had held a senior position on the board of the Prado before entering the diplomatic service.

They listened quietly as she explained the significance of the golden eagle.

She outlined its history, beginning with the old Conquistador, Sebastian Alfonzo de Martinez, not failing to mention she was a direct descendant, and finishing with the story of how they had found it at the old cabin site in the Jura. She did not mention the Mossad, or the old *Obersturmbannführer* Rolo Giessner, the *Reischwald*, or the involvement of the Israeli embassy. When she had finished, both gazed at her in wonderment.

'What do you want from us?' asked the Ambassador.

'We want three things from you, and I expect such undertakings as a Spanish citizen and the lawful custodian of the golden eagle:

'First: you will take custody of it and see someone takes it securely to the Government in *Madrid*, where it will be held in the utmost secrecy and security.

'Second: The Spanish Government will determine the true ownership of the statue. I want a say in this procedure.

'Third: I want my fiancé Mr Brodie to be recognised as much as I am for the recovery of this important piece of Muisica history.'

The Ambassador and his colleague sat back in their chairs and applauded. 'Bravo!' said the Cultural Attaché. 'You are a most formidable young woman, *Señorita,* and you have told us a remarkable story. I think we must agree with you.' She turned to Mike. '*Señor* Brodie, do you have any idea what you have in this lovely young woman? Truly, she is beyond pearls!'

Mike smiled. 'I think I have died and gone to heaven,' he said. 'No man is luckier than I am.'

'Well,' said the ambassador. 'We must look at this treasure. When can we see it?'

'Right now.' Maria reached for the backpack on the floor beside her chair. She took out the magnificent bird and placed it on the desk. '*¡Madre de Dios!*' said the ambassador. 'This must be worth the budget of a small country. Why do you even think of giving it away?'

Maria smiled. 'My illustrious ancestor stole it from its original owners,' she said. 'It has caused much sorrow and death ever since. I would like to see it go back whence it came.'

'Well,' he said, 'We will conform to your wishes. When do you expect to be back in Madrid?'

She looked at Mike. 'Not for several weeks,' she said. 'We are about to start our honeymoon!'

# FOR EVER AND EVER

It took them six weeks. They could not bear the thought of parting. Maria telephoned the University and explained her situation. They were not happy, for she had not even started her teaching, but they deferred to her wishes. Mike telephoned his brothers. 'Go for it, mate,' said Phil. 'We don't need you here. But promise you will bring this girl home for a while. It seems you have really struck gold at last.' He didn't know the irony in his words.

Once or twice a week, they took some of the cash to a bank and had it transferred to several accounts they both had at home. It took almost five weeks to do it. Mike reckoned they had at least two million dollars. 'Well,' he said one night, 'we won't have to worry about where our next meal is coming from!'

Maria said, 'I have imagined what we might do with that amount of money. Perhaps you would like a small villa on the Costa Brava. We would be close to Barcelona and my family.' Mike was noncommittal.

Each night they made love as if there would be no next time. Neither could get enough of each other. He revelled in her soft skin and lovely body she offered to him without reservation. She took him to new highs, as he did for her. Her flashing eyes, generous mouth and her obvious enjoyment drove him on and on. He knew he could not live without her. But he had to admit that he had his fill of bustling Europe.

Sometimes he longed for the wide-open plains of Brodie's Crossing, the soft summer nights, and the calls of all the familiar birds, the scent of eucalyptus oil and smoke from the bushfires on the scorching summer days. He thought with relish of the wide sandy beaches and the sparkling blue Pacific Ocean.

He missed the harvest, when giant machines toiled throughout the night and the rivers of golden grain flowed into bin, truck and silo. He missed the early morning rides through the calving cows in the late winter, when his horse's hooves crunched on the frost and its breath rose like steam from its nostrils, and the exhilarating gallops in the early morning, when he would arrive at the homestead, flushed and excited and hungry.

He was a son of this great southern land. He had worn its uniform, had fought bravely in its name. Like all Australian farmers, he had an elemental attachment to his land. Mike remembered his youth on 'Donegal' sitting on a hillside, his horse nuzzling his shoulder, watching the cattle string out along their tracks, heading for the water holes in the creek below. He could forsake none of this. He told Maria of his feelings.

She looked at him with love in her eyes. 'Mike, I know. Every Australian I have met feels the same way. You have a wonderful country and I want to be part of it too, but I have my own attachments. There must be a way we can have both. I cannot live without you, and I know you feel the same way. We will find a way.'

When they returned to Madrid, the government granted them an audience with the *Ministro de Cultura*, greeted warmly in the palatial offices in Madrid. It thrilled the minister, what Maria had accomplished, but there were some reservations.

'The Government,' he said, 'is divided on this issue. Someone has valued the statue conservatively at over one hundred million US Dollars. This is a substantial sum and disparate interests have bombarded us. There are those who say it is rightfully Spain's, seized in the name of the King. Others say that we should return it to that area of Columbia where it was found. The problem with that is there is no way to validate any claim to ownership, and if we give it to the Government of Colombia, the President or other corrupt officials might well appropriate it. You have made your position well known.

I cannot promise you anything, but I believe it will be given to the Museum of the Americas in Madrid or the National Museum of Colombia. Before it will be given to Colombia, they must satisfy the Government that it will always remain the property of the Colombian people. If it is to go there, we will require the Colombian Government to sign a treaty with Spain that will guarantee this.'

They accepted this decision. It was out of their hands now, and perhaps that was a good thing. They had plenty of money, and both agreed that too much money was likely not a good thing.

# EPILOGUE

'El Mundo' Madrid, 21 Jan 1996
El águila de oro
Madrid: The Spanish Government announced today that a valuable Muisica statue of a golden eagle stolen by Conquistadors in 1530 would be returned to Colombia. The statue had been the subject of much discussion since its discovery last year in France by a Spanish citizen Maria Isabella Martinez de Paloma, a prominent historian. Ms Martinez is thought to be ...

'El Mundo' Madrid, 31 Jan 1996
Medal for historian
Madrid: Historian Maria Isabella Martinez de Paloma, finder of the golden eagle statue, has been awarded the Orden Civil de Alfonso X el Sabio for contributions to History. Ms Martinez, currently visiting Australia, was unavailable for comment last night. The award ...

'El Tiempo' Bogata, 22 June 1996
Famous eagle arrives from Spain
Bogata: The fabulous eagle statue returned by Spain arrived today amongst some of the tightest security seen since last year's Presidential election. The statue, destined for the National Museum ...

'El Periódico de Catalunya' Barcelona July 1996
Prominent historian to wed.
Palómas: Maria Isabella Martinez de Paloma, who became famous for the discovery of the fabled golden eagle, will marry her Australian fiancé Mike Brodie in Barcelona this week. We believe that they have purchased a secluded villa on the Costa Brava where …

'The Brodie's Crossing Weekly' 26 July 1966
Local man to marry Spanish beauty
Barcelona: Mike Brodie, formerly proprietor of Brodie's Agricultural Services, has advised his family that he is to marry the Spanish aristocrat Maria Isabella Martinez de Paloma, whom he met recently on a tour of Europe. The newlyweds will return to Australia after a brief visit to South America. We do not know …

'The Times of London' 11 Sept 1996
Couple to be honoured by Colombian government
Bogata: Recent reports state that Mr and Mrs Mike Brodie are to be honoured by the Government of Colombia after the couple returned an ancient Muisica icon they had found in France last year to that country. Both will receive the *Orden de San Carlos* in a ceremony in Bogata later this month. The award is one of Colombia's highest awards to civilians and comes with a grant of more than $100,000. No information is to hand about the future of the couple, but Mr Brodie is an Australian farmer…

'New York Times' 21 Nov 1996
Multi-million dollar statue missing
Bogata: News just in from our South American correspondent says that a golden eagle statue, found last year by the famous Spanish historian Maria Isabella Martinez de Paloma, has disappeared from the country's national museum. Police say a glass display cabinet had been broken, but there was no evidence of forcible entry to the building.

The statue, believed to be worth over one hundred million dollars, was held under the most rigorous security. There is speculation that one or more of the security detail may have been involved. One curious aspect is the discovery of feathers on ...

## 'El Tiempo' Bogata, 12 Jan 1997
### Has el condor returned?

Cordoba: There have been reports from this area of livestock losses by Andean farmers in recent weeks. One farmer, Julio Ruiz, said that all the losses were similar. It had attacked the animals around the head. Their eyes were missing, and great strips of flesh torn from their cheeks. Señor Ruiz is reported as saying that his grandfather used to talk of such things when *condors* roamed the mountains, but they had seen none of these birds for almost fifty years. An unconfirmed report alleges that a teenage boy had seen the silhouette of an enormous bird fly across the face of the full moon. Ornithologists are ...

## 'New York Times' 28 April 1997
### Nazi war criminal sentenced to death

Tel Aviv: Former *SS* Lt. Colonel Rolo Giessner was found guilty by a court in Tel Aviv yesterday and sentenced to be hanged. Giessner, responsible for the execution of more than forty thousand Polish, Russian and Ukrainian Jews in 1941 and 1942, was the commander of one of the Nazi death squads called *Einsatzgruppen*; he ordered shot to death thousands of Jews, forcing them to dig their own graves before ...

## 'News of the World' London, 20 March 1997
### Scientists discover new form of leprosy.

Chicago: Medical researchers have discovered a hitherto unknown and extremely rare form of the ancient disease, leprosy. They report it is a particularly aggressive strain, with the typical necrosis proceeding at a rate over ten times faster than normal. Sufferers typically experience rapid weight loss followed by skin and tissue sloughing off. It may only take a matter of weeks before the muscle tissue comes away. Death follows quickly.

Dr Karl Guzmann of the Austrian Medical Institute, who was a leading member of the research team, said that this may explain similar symptoms reported in the Middle Ages, at that time considered the result of curses placed on people by gypsies and witches. Further studies will ...

## 'Donegal', Brodie's Crossing, NSW, Australia

Mike and Maria sat on the veranda of the homestead and listened to the cicadas begin their nightly concert. There was a full moon bathing the trees with a silver light; they could see some possums playing in a big gum tree near the cattle yards.

The watercourse behind the house throbbed with the chorus of frogs calling urgently for mates. They had millions of tadpoles to make and limited time in which to do it. The soft velvet night held them in its cloak.

'Oh Mike,' she said, 'It is so peaceful here. Now I know why you love this place so much. I want to be with you here forever, but I cannot. I have my new grant to write a treatise on South American Iconography. What can we do?'

'Well, I have my place here on the farm. My father left me a thousand acres that I have been leasing to the others. I plan to build a small house and spend some time here, giving Phil and the others a hand. But there is no reason to stay here all year. We have our villa in Spain, we have enough money to do what we want. We can spend our time in both places, even South America, if you want to go there. I always wanted to be the pampered companion of someone famous.'

'Then we will do that. It is settled. Now, let us seal our contract. Tonight, I yearn for the volcano again!'

He looked at her with wonder, at her beautiful eyes, her trim body, her soft skin and her luscious hair and knew he would live in heaven forever.

Shawline Publishing Group Pty Ltd
www.shawlinepublishing.com.au

Milton Keynes UK
Ingram Content Group UK Ltd.
UKHW040643210824
447168UK00002B/21